Samuel French Acting Edition

I0591832

Goodnight, Tyler

Written by B.J. Tindal

Developmental Dramaturgy by
Maansi Sahay Seth

SAMUELFRENCH.COM   SAMUELFRENCH.CO.UK

MUSIC USE NOTE

Licensees are solely responsible for obtaining formal written permission from copyright owners to use copyrighted music in the performance of this play and are strongly cautioned to do so. If no such permission is obtained by the licensee, then the licensee must use only original music that the licensee owns and controls. Licensees are solely responsible and liable for all music clearances and shall indemnify the copyright owners of the play(s) and their licensing agent, Samuel French, against any costs, expenses, losses and liabilities arising from the use of music by licensees. Please contact the appropriate music licensing authority in your territory for the rights to any incidental music.

IMPORTANT BILLING AND CREDIT REQUIREMENTS

If you have obtained performance rights to this title, please refer to your licensing agreement for important billing and credit requirements.

GOODNIGHT, TYLER was originally developed by Quick Silver Theater Company in New York, New York (Tyrone Henderson, Founder; Lizan Mitchell, Co-founder).

GOODNIGHT, TYLER received its world premiere at the Alliance Theatre (Susan V. Booth, Jennings Hertz Artistic Director; Mike Schleifer, Managing Director) in Atlanta, Georgia on February 21, 2019. The performance was directed by Kent Gash, with assistant direction by Ibi Owolabi. The stage manager was Wendy Palmer and the assistant stage manager was Allison Kelly. The cast was as follows:

TYLER EVANS . . . . .Travis Turner

DAVIS JENSEN. . . . . .Alex Gibson

FANNIE EVANS . . . . Andrea Frye

CHELSEA NOTLEY. . . . . Alexandra Ficken

SHANA HARRIS. . . . . Danielle Deadwyler

DREW MILLER . . . . .Chris Harding

CHARACTERS

TYLER EVANS – Black. 26 years old. Gentle, goofy, determined, flustered, simple, and nerdy. He knows what it means to fight and say, "I love you" at the same time.

DAVIS JENSEN – White. 26 years old. Nurturing, dramatic, anxious, lonely, funny, and sarcastic. He gives endlessly to the things that are important to him, but fears being left behind.

FANNIE EVANS – Black. 76 years old. Relaxed, cocky, silly, fresh, stubborn, and caring. She is a teacher in the way she has learned to live alone without ever being lonely.

CHELSEA NOTLEY – White. 27 years old. Intellectual, kind, stressed, determined, loyal, and imaginative. She struggles to balance what she wants for herself with what she needs for herself.

SHANA HARRIS – Black. 19 years old. Logical, passionate, impatient, empathetic, intelligent...smart-ass. She's tired of waiting for other people to understand her anger.

DREW MILLER – White. 25 years old. Excited, defensive, hyper-masculine, jealous, loving, and scared. He treats friendship like an infinite celebration, and never wants it to be forgotten.

ACKNOWLEDGMENTS

This story exists because of the community of storytellers, thinkers, organizers, musicians, and mentors that cared for it. From my undergrad adviser, Caroline Jackson Smith, to my mother, Gail Scott, I am deeply grateful for every village that helped tell this story...

To Axandre Oge, Colin Anderson, Amara Granderson, Katy Early, Calypso Simone, Evan Board, Amethyst Carey, Dominique Pearson, Alison Kronstadt, and Arianna Crawford, for getting your hands dirty... doing the messy, brave, and hilarious work it takes to tell a sad story for the first time.

To Kent Gash, Travis Turner, Alex Gibson, Andrea Frye, Alexandra Ficken, Danielle Deadwyler, Chris Harding, and Ibi Owolabi, for committing to creating the wildest and strongest world imaginable.

To Cezar Williams, Malik Ali, Ethan Dubin, Elizabeth Van Dyke, Marianna McClellan, Jasmine Rush, Michael Fell, and Tyrone Henderson, for teaching us to "be as funny as we are smart."

To Christopher Betts, Jaysen Wright, Joshua Simon, Kim James Bey, Joey Rose, Shannon Dorsey, Matthew Alan Ward, Celise Kalke, and Josiah Turner, for challenging each character to be more human, even when it's ugly.

To Maansi, my partner, for every magic carpet ride, in and out of every village.

And especially, to the living family members of Sandra Bland, Rekia Boyd, Philando Castile, Michael Brown, Trayvon Martin, Tamir Rice, and the countless other Black children whose lives have been taken by police violence, thank you for continuing to love despite, and for always teaching me what a miracle it is to be both Black and Alive.

Thanks,

B.J.

ACT ONE

Scene One
Present

(In the dark we hear the needle of a record player, and a jazz standard begins to play.[*] It's not creepy though. More comforting and familiar as lights slowly rise on a dark apartment living room.)

(It's 3:00 a.m. This is the apartment of two mid-twenty-somethings. A kitchen with an island. Random laundry and empty glasses sprinkled on the floor and armchair. Conflicting aesthetics all over the damn place. DAVIS is asleep on the couch. He fell asleep with his glasses on and with a book over his face because he's an #intellectual.)

(Music stops abruptly. TYLER bursts through the door in a panic. He's breathing heavily. He's looking around the room, anxious, a little confused, maybe even scared. He lives here, but it's almost as if he's seeing it for the first time. With his back to DAVIS, he says:)

TYLER. Davis? ...Are you awake?

(DAVIS is not awake. This does not stop TYLER.)

I uhh... I think I died tonight. I wasn't planning on it happening, and I swear I didn't even do anything

---

*A license to produce *Goodnight, Tyler* does not include a performance license for any third-party or copyrighted music. Licensees should create an original composition or use music in the public domain. For further information, please see Music Use Note on page 3.

wrong! I did everything Grandma told me I should do, but I'm pretty sure – well, actually, I know for sure I died tonight. One minute I was on the ground and then... I saw my body and everything! And it was definitely dead. There was no life there, it – ...it was just a body. ...And don't get me wrong, I liked it for the most part! I always worry that my head's not proportional to the rest of my figure, but it actually looks kind of okay! I just – ...wasn't in it. So yeah. I'm very dead. ...Grandma's gonna be mad.

You'll tell her for me, yeah? Because when I was looking at it I realized...it's just a body! It can't move, or dance, or do any impressions... And...I think I saw what everyone sees. Well, the people who don't know me anyway. They see me on the street and sometimes I'm just a heavy...ashy, dark body. I mean you look at it, and it doesn't smile, or joke. It's still. So who's to say it ever smiled, or joked, or won any spelling bees! ...Four spelling bees!! Who's to say it ever did anything? ...So it's kind of, well, useless...isn't it? Disposable, maybe. Because just looking at it lying there it can't...prove anything! ...I mean, that's how this works, right?

...No. No no no no way, I can't just leave behind some – some body! It's just a body! And while it's handsome and generally nimble, that's all it is! And at the very least I would like to make sure that I'm not just...a dead body.

> *(Pause.)*

...I think I'm worth more than that.

> (**DAVIS** *gives a disapproving/sleepy/"I will literally murder you" kinda groan.*)

...Are you serious?!

DAVIS. *(Without lifting his head.)* I'm asleep.

TYLER. My dead spirit is trying to communicate with you, and you're asleep. Don't you think that's a little rude?

DAVIS. Don't you think delivering a soliloquy while I'm trying to sleep is a lot rude?

TYLER. Not if you're lying on the beach with Jesse Williams again.

DAVIS. *(Closing his eyes tighter.)* He HAPPENS to be rubbing my body down in coconut oil, not that it's any of your business –

TYLER. *(Running around the room on a mission.)* We need to hide all my puppy calendars!

DAVIS. Ohhhh he's getting further and further –

TYLER. Also how do you delete the Google history on an iPhone?

DAVIS. Tyler, I'm about to check my watch, and if it is anywhere near the time I think –

TYLER. Shut up for two seconds and help me!

DAVIS. *(Sits up and takes a deep breath.)* ...Why now?

TYLER. Because I'm dead now!!

DAVIS. Ahh, right. You're "dead."

TYLER. Yes. I'm dead. I died.

DAVIS. Well can you go be dead in your room please? Silently?

TYLER. I'm being serious. We need to start collecting stuff and putting it all in order before we run out of time, it's important!

> *(He is rushing about the room in a headless chicken kinda way when* **DAVIS** *cuts his path off.)*

DAVIS. ...Tyler, look at me.

> *(***TYLER*** *looks.)*

What did you do?

TYLER. What do you mean?

DAVIS. I mean it's three a.m. and you're babbling incoherently. What did you do?

TYLER. I didn't do anything! Are you gonna help me or not?

DAVIS. Were you out drinking? Did you puke on another bartender?

TYLER. Why do you automatically assume that I DID something?

DAVIS. Well, am I wrong?

TYLER. That's not the point! Can't I just be dead? Like, damn! Get your priorities straight!

DAVIS. And what's that supposed to mean?

TYLER. It means, my Black dead body is lying out there, and the first thing you say is, "What did you do?" Really?

DAVIS. Ohhh heeeerrre we go –

TYLER. We are preserving the dead Black man's legacy!!

DAVIS. I'm not having a political debate at three in the morning. Did you do something or not?

TYLER. ...FINE!

So I did something. WHATever! But I "did something," and THEN I DIED, which means I'm not going to get to do ANYTHING for a long-LONG time. Like EVER-long-long time. So can't you just be a normal best friend, sob over my carcass, and do whatever the hell my lingering spirit tells you to do?

DAVIS. How about this? I'm going to go to sleep, and when you and your "lingering spirit" are ready to talk about whatever it is you did, I'll be wai–

TYLER. Davis you really can't go to bed now!!

DAVIS. Why not?

TYLER. I just TOLD YOU!!

DAVIS. Yes, okay, "you're dead" but what's the subtext here? Are you stressed out about something? I mean I thought maybe you'd calm down for like two seconds now that you get to marry –

(Stops.)

Oh God, did you?

TYLER. Did I what?

DAVIS. Where is Chelsea?

TYLER. That doesn't matter right now, she's fine –

DAVIS. You sent your "new fiancée" to walk home by herself?

TYLER. What, no!! That's not what happened.

DAVIS. If I call her right now –

TYLER. OKAY WAIT NO DON'T!!

> *(They look at each other.)*

...Yeah um...it's complicated?

DAVIS. I knew it. You ruined it!!

TYLER. I didn't –

DAVIS. Ya make me look like a complete asshole in front of her, and you still found a way to ruin it!! Incredible. What'd you do, did you freak her out with your Louis Armstrong impression again?

TYLER. That wasn't even what we fought about!!

DAVIS. And now you're freaking out because you think you've ruined the one chance you might have at love, blah blah.

> *(Picking up the phone and dialing.)*

Bullshit. You can't stay engaged for a day but **I** can't marry Jesse Williams?? It's bullsh–

TYLER. What are you doing?

DAVIS. I'm fixing it.

TYLER. *(Running/almost tackling* **DAVIS**.*)* No no no, you can't – she – I think she cracked it when the shot went off.

DAVIS. When the – ...I'm sorry, what?

TYLER. I know I know she doesn't have a phone case, I tried to tell her, but she lives a reckless lifestyle –

DAVIS. Stop it. What shot? What are you –

TYLER. I was shot. That's why I'm dead.

DAVIS. *(Looks at* **TYLER**.*)* ...Right. I'm going to bed.

TYLER. *(Calling after* **DAVIS**.*)* Still don't believe me? FINE! Wait for it then. They'll call any minute!

DAVIS. Who?!

TYLER. THE POLICE!

DAVIS. "THE POLI–" ...you got in trouble with the police?!

TYLER. Well yeah you could say that.

DAVIS. And you ran? Why the hell would you do that? Are they looking for you?

TYLER. No I don't think they need to since they totally shot me.

DAVIS. They – ...What? Why would they shoot at you?

TYLER. Because they were aiming at the nice "yoga" instructor walking out of the Whole Foods across the street and they missed. Why the hell do you think Davis?

DAVIS. You don't even know how to run anymore! The only reason you would be running is if –

TYLER. The police were being professional killers and I was being professionally Black?

DAVIS. *(Pause. His face changes.)* ...This isn't seriously about –

TYLER. I wasn't going to say anything, but now that you bring it up –

DAVIS. I swear to God, you go to one Black Lives Matter rally and suddenly you think you're Stokely Carmichael.

TYLER. I'm not trying to lead a movement. I would just like to get my stuff ready for my damn mourners!

DAVIS. Will you just –

> *(Phone rings. He looks at it. It's creepy.)*

...Is this like some "pop-up-die-in-awareness-guerilla-theater-THING" you're trying to prove a point with?!

TYLER. Davis –

DAVIS. *(Slams phone down. He has had enough.)* Well, I'm sorry, Tyler. Okay? There. I'm sorry. I'm sorry I didn't wanna go to one of your anti-capitalist coalition anarchist protest rallies with you in the dead of January. I'm sorry about racism and "the Prison Industrial Complex" and all of the other shitty socio-political whatchamacallits you learned about from your little friends LITERALLY THREE WEEKS AGO, but I can't solve racism at three in the morning.

TYLER. I'm not asking you to –

DAVIS. So to wake me up and try to guilt me with some elaborate played out scheme is uncalled for. And bratty! It's a bunch of uppity, entitled, leftist-wannabe crap, and I'm not putting up with it tonight!!

TYLER. I didn't get myself shot to make you feel guilty, Davis.

DAVIS. Goodnight Tyler.

(*Phone rings.*)

I'm not picking it up. I'm going to sleep.

(*He turns to go to bed.*)

TYLER. (*Plays his last card.*) WES CRAVEN WOULD BE ASHAMED!!

DAVIS. (*Too far.*) ...ExCUSE ME?!

TYLER. The horror movie formula is the same every time Davey. We both know the idiot in the beginning of the horror movie should never do the thing! "Don't go into the dark basement. Don't have premarital sex in an abandoned warehouse. Don't abandon your dead best friend in the living room!!"

DAVIS. How dare you! I am NOT –

TYLER. It's ironic, isn't it? Usually the idiot is a humorful Black man. And here I am, Black and dead and comical as hell, and yet YOU still get to play the idiot who's gonna do the thing!! My God, I can't have anything!!

DAVIS. OKAY FINE! You wanna bring the entire horror genre into this? Cool. But I'm disappointed, "Ty-bear." You of all people should know this "death" you came up with for yourself is unrealistic.

TYLER. Unrealistic?

DAVIS. Yes. See, when YOU die, it'll be because you tripped in those Nikes you bought three sizes up to overcompensate and fell down an elevator shaft! Or maybe you'll have a heart attack when you find out they canceled the *Real Housewives*.

TYLER. *(Under his breath.)* That's uncalled for.

DAVIS. AND NOW I AM GOING TO BED!

> *(Phone rings.)*

Dammit, I swear if that phone rings again –

TYLER. *(Now he's mad.)* So what? ...You don't think police officers shoot people like me?

DAVIS. Answer the phone!

TYLER. Why? Why not me, Davis?

DAVIS. Take the damn phone, Tyler!

TYLER. What, am I not Black enough to shoot?

DAVIS. You're being an idiot!

TYLER. No. I'm being dead! Because a racist-ass police system killed me. Now honor my life, dammit, or I swear I will haunt the shit out of you!

> *(The phone continues to ring. **DAVIS** and **TYLER** stare at each other/have a face-off moment over the ringing. **DAVIS** gives in, turns away from **TYLER** to answer the phone. **TYLER** exits slowly.)*

DAVIS. *(Answers the phone.)* Who the hell is this?!

> *(Beat.)*

...Slow down I can't... – Chelsea?

> *(Beat.)*

What's wrong? You're really not making any – ...hold on –

> *(Puts phone down to turn to **TYLER**.)*

Why is she crying? What did you – Tyler? ...Tyler? *(Phone.)* Chelsea, hold on he was right here a second ago, you can – ...his body? What are you – but he's –

> *(Puts phone down again.)*

(Calling offstage.) Tyler you have to talk to her. I can't stop her from crying!

(Phone.) Just wait a minute, okay? He's coming...no...
I – ...Chelsea, I swear he was just here. He was just –
(Calling offstage again.) Tyler, I'm serious!! ...

> *(No response. He waits. With a little more desperation:)*

...TYLER!

> *(No response.)*

> *(He frantically runs offstage to find Tyler. Salty.)*

Scene Two
Two Months Ago

(After a few very small moments of an empty stage, lights go up brighter than they were before. We happy now.)

*(***CHELSEA*** enters through the front door stage right. **TYLER** is behind her carrying a box. The two have been bickering for what has probably been forty-five minutes, just like so...)*

TYLER. But why can't we just –

CHELSEA. 'Cause I don't wanna start –

TYLER. We wouldn't even have to –

CHELSEA. You keep saying that like I care about that –

TYLER. I care about that –

CHELSEA. Well maybe you should care less about that and care more about –

TYLER. How is that even related to –!!

CHELSEA. Because you won't eve–

TYLER. YOU won't even!!

CHELSEA. I DID SO EVEN!! It's your turn to even –

TYLER. Well if I have to you have to too!! You're being stubborn.

CHELSEA. Well I'd rather be stubborn than a literal child.

(They both sit on the couch in a huff, arms folded, looking away from each other...like literal children. Neither will budge, but then:)

TYLER. ...I'm just saying very few people get their engagement photos taken at the Renaissance faire and it'd be very original of us if we were to –

CHELSEA. WE ARE NOT GETTING MARRIED!!

TYLER. *(Placing his box down beside the couch.)* Come on, if you really didn't want to marry me, would we even still be having this debate? I'm young, I'm attractive, I practically have two jobs!

CHELSEA. Managing an online World of Warcraft forum is not a job, sweetheart. It's a condition.

TYLER. It's my duty to my country!

CHELSEA. Well maybe if you would just CONSIDER looking at –

TYLER. I AM NOT GOING TO BUSINESS SCHOOL!

CHELSEA. But come on, think about it for a second: CEO. Penthouse office. Your own rolly chair! You could OWN World of Warcraft!

TYLER. Please. I already own them. I'm the best there ever was.

CHELSEA. See! Right there!! We both know you don't want to spend all of eternity as a coffee barista when you could run your own balloon-animal company!

TYLER. I told you that in confidence!!

CHELSEA. And I told YOU that having a ten-year plan is very helpful –

TYLER. Pleeeeassse not the ten-year plan agai–

CHELSEA. For example, I graduate from college, spend two years building my resume, return to grad school where I'm in a three-year program to complete my dissertation on the Spice Girls comeback tour then spend four years as a "Feminist, Gender, and Sexuality" professor at some small obscure liberal arts college where I'll develop a serious case of baby fever and marry the first man with a fixed jawline who will take me! Who is also shorter than me. And is a doctor... If you fulfill the requirements then, then I suppoooose –

(Poking at him.)

TYLER. *(Waving her off playfully.)* Okay okay I get it.

CHELSEA. *(Taking his hand.)* I'm just saying it's okay to want things for yourself, Tyler! God, I mean, you do everything dude!! Like-uh-like...like those college kids you work with now! You'd make an amazing teacher! Spend three years in a Master's program and you can teach wherever you want! Just for a second, think about thirty-six-year-old Tyler Evans! Where is he?

TYLER. Married to you.

CHELSEA. *(Thumbs up, walks out.)* Great. See you tomorrow.

TYLER. Seriously seriously! Just, just look at me for a second.

(He cups her face a little.)

I love you. And I don't mean it in an "I'm-gonna-get-lucky-after-prom" kinda way. More like in a "seventy-five-years-old-and-stuck-in-this-until-I-die-in-my-sleep"...kinda way. Don't you feel the same way?

CHELSEA. You're good company.

TYLER. GOOD ENOUGH!

(Score!)

Look, we both know this sort of thing doesn't happen anymore in our generation. Normally one of us has severe daddy issues or is a little uglier than the other one. I am in love with you. I want to spend the rest of my life with you –

CHELSEA. What? You don't think I get that? Of course I love you! Of course I wanna...you know...wake up next to you every day in an adorable little house in Maine on the water raising two kids and my cat together, whatever! But – ...I'm not... I'm not done yet, Tyler. You can get that, right? I mean, you're not done either!

TYLER. It's not "the end" of anything though, it would just be the start of something! Come on, would you please just consider making a new plan that fits both of us in?

(He gives her the puppy dog eyes. She cracks a smile...but no.)

CHELSEA. ...Your grandmother hates me!!

TYLER. She doesn't "hate" you.

CHELSEA. I swear to God, she tried to snip a lock of my hair before we left today! The woman is basically your mother, and I'm pretty sure she has a doll of me that she sticks needles into at night.

TYLER. My grandma doesn't hate anyone. She's just... protective...in a creative way.

CHELSEA. And Drew?

TYLER. Drew adores you!

CHELSEA. Yah, I've noticed. That's kind of the problem. We would totally have to adopt him! And I'm sorry, but I don't want a misogynistic rugby frat star peeing on my carpet every night.

TYLER. That was one time!!

CHELSEA. And don't even get me started on Davis!

TYLER. What about Davis??

CHELSEA. I know how this works: I marry you, I marry him. I am not marrying him. The boy flosses on a schedule. Who flosses regularly?? And more importantly, you marry me, he marries me. And he's not marrying me. He hates me the most.

TYLER. You're being paranoid.

CHELSEA. Oh don't give me that. I wasn't born yesterday. I've seen Steve Harvey.

TYLER. ...What does that even – look. You don't have to worry about Davis. He'll get on board.

CHELSEA. "He'll get on board"? I'm not a staged coup, Tyler. You're missing the point. Sure. It's not the end of anything but...it's the beginning of the "rest of your life." No one's ready for that. I'm not. They're not. They don't – ...they barely want me here now. Especially not Davis!

TYLER. He's a big boy. He can take care of himself

      (**DAVIS** *bursts through the front door in great turmoil.*)

DAVIS. Tyler I need you!

TYLER. What is it Davey?!

DAVIS. I just had the world's most catastrophically awful day! Get out *P.S. I Love You.* We're ordering Domino's and getting emotionally fucked up tonight.

TYLER. Oh God. What happened?!

DAVIS. Well you wouldn't believe how –

    *(He notices **CHELSEA**.)*

Ohh, Chelsea. I'm sorry I didn't realize I was interrupting.

CHELSEA. No, it's okay. Hi Davis…bad day?

DAVIS. I…nope! No no, I'm sorry. You're having Chyler time! I really don't wanna talk about it anyway.

CHELSEA. Well thank you, that's very –

DAVIS. *(Collapsing between the two.)* Okay, but like I'm sitting at my desk, waiting for Patrick Greenbaum to finish his lunch so I can finally go on my break.

TYLER. Ugh. "Patrick Greenbaum."

DAVIS. Yeah, I know, here we go. And there's this huge meeting going on so someone has to cover the front desk until "Patrick Greenbaum" gets back from some gluten-free farmer's market no one's ever heard of. And on top of that, he left the empty cup from his fifteenth green smoothie of the day next to my computer, so I toss it in the trash. Meanwhile, I am LITERALLY starving. So then he finally comes back from his break, no less than sixteen minutes late mind you, notices the smoothie cup is gone, and actually accuses me of drinking it.

TYLER. Which doesn't make any sense, because who the hell would ever drink something like that?

DAVIS. I KNOW! So I'm like, "No Patrick, as hard as it is for you to believe, I did not drink your earthy crunchy smoothie full of…leaves and shit!!" All while, keep in mind, I'm all but about to faint from malnourishment. And then he comes in in his boat shoes –

TYLER. In those fucking boat shoes??

DAVIS. In those fucking boat shoes!! And he actually says, "I bet you got tired of your Burger King fries and wanted something healthy."

CHELSEA. HA-HA! That's ridiculous, I mean who would eat Burger King fries, right?

DAVIS. *(What is wrong with her?)* ...Well hopefully everyone.

TYLER. Everyone, Chelsea.

DAVIS. Everyone. Anyway, then just as I'm starting to see spots, because at this point, still only had one donut all day, Patrick calls our boss out of the meeting and ACTUALLY files a formal complaint about my "inability to collaborate." I'm never gonna make employee of the month now. I told you working at BuzzFeed was a mistake.

TYLER. Ugh "Patrick." Who does he think he is? With his beard.

DAVIS. And his white-boy dreads.

TYLER. And his gauges.

CHELSEA. We are not getting married.

TYLER. Wait wait wait, hold on!

CHELSEA. I'm ALWAYS holding on! Because it's ALWAYS Dyler time!

DAVIS. Oh God, honey, no no of course not. It's called "Tavis" time, "Dyler" time would be weird.

CHELSEA. *(Deep breath/low-key resisting the urge to wrap her hands around* **DAVIS**' *neck.)* I'm grabbing my things from your room and then I'm going home. You boys enjoy your movie.

DAVIS. *(Waits until* **CHELSEA** *is completely out of sight.)* Absolutely not!

TYLER. Davis, please!

DAVIS. You can't marry her! You marry her, I marry her. I'm not marrying her. I've seen Steve Harvey.

TYLER. I don't understand why –!! We have been together for almost two years now. What did you think was going to happen?

DAVIS. That the spark in your relationship would fizzle, she'd cheat on you with a Norwegian model, then after a year and a half of heartbreak, you'd have a chance meeting with Emma Watson, and we'd marry her instead. The seven-year plan?

TYLER. I swear to God...

DAVIS. I'm just saying, we can do better.

TYLER. I don't want better! I want Chelsea. Chelsea makes ME better!

DAVIS. Like it's not enough already that you're starting college over.

TYLER. I'm not "starting college over." The Black Student Union asked the community for volunteers, and I told you I want to start –

DAVIS. It just seems like a lot of change!! First you marry this scary woman. Next thing you know, ABC moves *Modern Family* an hour up. Which means we have to move Olive Garden night from Thursdays to Tuesdays, which doesn't even work for you because you have to play beer pong with a Black Student Union I would call rather aggressive –

TYLER. We don't play beer pong.

DAVIS. You get married and become a Black Panther, and I have to cut breadsticks out of my diet. Is that what you want? You don't want little children to have free breadsticks and salad –

TYLER. *(Secret weapon.)* Clark Owens.

DAVIS. Hey! Don't bring Clark into this!

TYLER. What did I do when you were too shy to ask your first boyfriend's name?

DAVIS. ...You asked him for me.

TYLER. And when you were too shy to ask him on a date?

DAVIS. ...You asked him on a date for me.

TYLER. And when you were too shy to go on that date?

DAVIS. ...You went on the date for me...and told me whether or not he made that annoying teeth sucking sound at dinner.

TYLER. And you had six happy months together before the toenail thing! All because of me. I have been ride-or-die Davis since day one. Why can't you do the same for me?

DAVIS. I am!

TYLER. No! You're not. You're mocking me. Whether or not you get why I like to volunteer with Black students who are SMART and CRITICAL, you should support it because I say it's important to me. And it's the same thing with Chelsea! Maybe you don't like her very much or even if you think I'm being naïve, it doesn't matter! It should be enough when I tell you that she makes me very happy!

DAVIS. Well she makes ME very anxious.

TYLER. "Well" this isn't about you. This is about me.

(**CHELSEA** *enters again.*)

DAVIS. (*Challenge accepted.*) ...Fine. I can be supportive. Watch me.

(*To* **CHELSEA.**) Chelsea, I think you should marry us.

CHELSEA. ...What's about to happen?

DAVIS. I'm not gonna lie to you. You marry him you marry me. But I'm not so bad. I can tie a bowtie –

TYLER. And he goes to church sometimes!

DAVIS. Think about those weddings you'll start getting invited to. If Tyler gets sick, you can show me off to your sorority sisters instead. It's like having a back-up husband!

TYLER. A Vice Husband!

CHELSEA. Okay, very funny –

DAVIS. Then of course there is scenario B...where the best you can hope for is an extra three years of lonely Saturday nights watching reruns of *Roseanne*...

TYLER. Along with blind dates and "swiping right"...

DAVIS. Just waiting for that match with Jesse Williams because you thought you deserved to dream!

TYLER. But you'll be reminded you can **NEVER** dream, every Friday afternoon when your "work friends" offer to take you bowling –

DAVIS. And you start to feel obligated, because, sure, you could like bowling! You could be good at bowling!

TYLER. You could go bowling instead of being married. That's an option.

DAVIS. I just couldn't in good conscience watch you become a professional bowler without presenting you with the other offer.

DAVIS & TYLER. We're thinking of you!

> (**CHELSEA**, *freaked the hell out, stands still. Then she lets out a sigh and smiles at* **TYLER**. *She approaches him slowly and gives him a big [but soft] kiss on the mouth.*)

CHELSEA. ...I will see you tomorrow, love.

> (*Before closing the front door behind her, she turns and gives him a lil' wink.*)

TYLER. (*Score again!*) ...DID YOU SEE THAT? SHE WINKED!! SHE WINKED!! WHAT DO YOU THINK THAT MEANS?!

DAVIS. She has a twitch.

TYLER. (*Beginning to dance around the room.*) Ah ah ah! I know what it means! It means I'M going to be Mr. Mrs. Chelsea Notley!! Ohhhhhhhh this calls for a celebration.

> (*He opens one of the boxes next to the couch and pulls out a clunky, janky, dusty record player.*)

DAVIS. Your grandma didn't seriously give you that old thing, did she?

TYLER. Along with all of her records!

(He picks up a box and excitedly skips down the hallway.)

Oooo let's get drunk and dance to Ella Fitzgerald!!

(He begins making trumpet noises obnoxiously.)

DAVIS. *(Screaming over the noise.)* If you think I'm taking this other box upstairs for you, you're even more of a diva than I realized.

TYLER. IIIII can't hear you!!

DAVIS. Tyler! Tyler get back here!!

*(Lights shift to that sadder, more empty lighting immediately. **DAVIS** is still caught up in the moment of watching his friend disappear through the hallway. **CHELSEA** enters in different clothing.)*

Scene Three
Present Day

(**CHELSEA**'s *face is drained, probably from crying like everyone else. The sound of the door shutting behind her snaps* **DAVIS** *back to reality.*)

CHELSEA. It doesn't work...

DAVIS. Huh?

CHELSEA. I tried it already. Screaming at him to come back. But he doesn't come back. He's –

DAVIS. Dead... Right.

CHELSEA. ...I'm sorry. I should've knocked, I'm just so used to –

DAVIS. No no, it's fine...uhh... I just sort of spaced out for a second. Drew's already here actually.

CHELSEA. Okay, great, uh – I was actually hoping you and I could talk for a –

DAVIS. He and Ms. Evans should be down in a minute.

CHELSEA. *(Oh no!)* ...Ms. – ...Tyler's...she's here?

DREW. *(Stomping in from offstage like a moody teenager.)* She won't stop crying! I've tried everything. Do something!!

DAVIS. Drew...I thought I asked you not to leave her alone.

DREW. Well excuse me if I don't want my sweatshirt used as a snot rag! And besides, now she's doing, I don't know, "grandma-things" in there, like emptying all the candy from her pocketbook...which she won't even share with me!

(**FANNIE** *enters with awful wails and weeps and sobs. It's uncomfortable for everyone.*)

DAVIS. ...Ms. Evans? Are you oka– I mean...do you need anything?

FANNIE. *(Sniffling.)* No no please baby, don't worry 'bout me. By the way, you're out of toilet paper. Young man, can I see your sweatshirt again?

CHELSEA. Good morning Ms. Evans...

(Very uncomfortable silence.)

I – uh, sorry...I-I just wanted to say uh...I'm very sorry... for your loss.

(We're all uncomfortable.)

FANNIE. ...That's a nice sweater. Can I see it?

DAVIS. *(Interjecting quickly.)* Why doesn't everyone take a seat? I have his stuff right here to...start going through.

(He takes the box and topples it over.)

...This is pretty much everything I could find. I have a few empty boxes so people can take what they want. I figure we can all split it evenly.

(Everyone stares at the pile of stuff. They're paralyzed...)

CHELSEA. Wow...so this is everything. This is...all of it.

DREW. All of him...

DAVIS. All that's left, yeah.

CHELSEA. I guess I just thought there'd be more... I mean, he lived here, doesn't it seem like there should be more?

DREW. I told you I wanted to help gather things. But of course, your roommate is murdered, and you use it as an opportunity to grab all the good stuff before anyone else, right?

CHELSEA. Hey, uh, could we not –

DAVIS. What "good stuff"? Half his stuff is garbage.

DREW. Garbage?? Dude, don't talk about his stuff like that. He's dead.

CHELSEA. STOP! Just – ...can we stop using that word? Obviously he's – ...I don't think we need a reminder every five minutes, okay?

DREW. Fine. Whatever.

DAVIS. Okay, let's just...look at what's here...

(He half-heartedly picks up an old Sudoku book.)

DAVIS. What about this? It's a half-done Sudoku book. Anyone?

DREW. I don't think so.

DAVIS. I guess I can take it –

DREW. *(Snatches it.)* You know, actually, I think I'll take it.

CHELSEA. Oh, wow, he still has these dumb sunglasses? Haha…wow. I – uh, I actually would really love to take these, if you guys don't mind?

DREW. Fine with me.

DAVIS. Me too.

FANNIE. *(Sniff sniff.)* Let me see them?

> (**CHELSEA** *passes them carefully.*)

Aww these are precious. It reminds me of the ones he used to wear when he was a boy. I think I'll put them in my box actually.

CHELSEA. Oh…yeah… I mean, yes!

FANNIE. Just want a few of my grandson's things, you understand.

CHELSEA. Of course. Absolutely…obviously there's plenty of stuff to go around. Davis, did you find –

DREW. *(Doing the most.)* HERE! I'll help! There's plenty of stuff! Look there's his rock collection, and his baseball signed by Derek Jeter, and this…thing…

DAVIS. That was his dream catcher –

DREW. THANK YOU Davis! I know about his…"dream catcher." I don't need you to "identify" all of these things that are of which I already know! So why don't you just go bake a cake or something.

CHELSEA. Davis, you're giving his PlayStation away? You guys don't want it?

DAVIS. I never touch that thing anymore. It's just taking up space.

DREW. I don't need Davis' leftovers!

CHELSEA. Glad we're being mature about this… Well, cool, then I'd like to take it –

FANNIE. Tyler used to play those little game cartoons all day long. I remember I worked nine extra night shifts and sold my wedding ring at the pawn shop to buy him his first. Having it next to my rocking chair would be a treat.

CHELSEA. ...Ohh...uh – well I sort of –

DAVIS. Chels, you should – ...You know, 'cause –

CHELSEA. Right, duh, of course. It's the least I can do, Ms. Evans.

FANNIE. Thank you dear. Thank you Davis.

DREW. *(Nyeh nyeh.)* "Thank you Davis."
  (All up in **DAVIS**' *face.)* Please. Kiss more ass, I dare you.

DAVIS. I swear to God, Drew –

CHELSEA. OH! This was the watch he was wearing on our first date! He – haha – he uh...he told me if he had expensive jewelry on that I was statistically more likely to marry him for money... God, he's such a goob, I don't think he even wore watches like that... I'd really like to keep this –

FANNIE. Is that his watch? The $250 watch?

CHELSEA. ...Maybe.

FANNIE. I've been looking for a watch to wear for some time now, with my little old brain going in and out, I would love to have Tyler's to wear if I could.

CHELSEA. Ms. Evans, that sounds really lovely, but he wore this on our **first date**, and I –

FANNIE. I know I know dear, besides, with my elderly brittle wrists –

CHELSEA. I just think –

FANNIE. And my little ol' brain –

CHELSEA. Right, but –

FANNIE. But I'm sure it'll look nicer around those pretty little things you have.

CHELSEA. ...Okay here.

FANNIE. Aw sugar, thank yo–

CHELSEA. *(Over it.)* It's fine just take it.

DREW. Davis, where are the vinyl, ESPECIALLY well-insulated slippers *I* got him for his nineteenth birthday??

DAVIS. Leave me alone, I didn't see the –

DREW. OH REALLY?! Was there anything else you didn't see? Like his journals, or his bank account number or his underwear??

CHELSEA. Oh my God! Oh my God...these are the headphones I got him last Christmas...but he hated these things, why would he keep them? ...I can't believe he would do that. I...I have to keep them.

FANNIE. Let me see?

CHELSEA. *(Really??)* What? ...W-Why?

FANNIE. Oh they just look nice, that's all. Are these Beats by Dr. Dre?

CHELSEA. *(Can't hold it back anymore.)* ...What possible interest could you have in a pair of $100 headphones? You're like eighty.

DAVIS. Chelsea!

CHELSEA. *(Shit!)* Sorry! I don't know where that came from!

FANNIE. Did I do something to upset you?

CHELSEA. It's not that, it's just – ...maybe there's something else in here you'll like better, yeah? Here, I'll help you find something.

FANNIE. I'm pretty fixed on the headphones.

CHELSEA. Ms. Evans –

DAVIS. Here, maybe it's best if the headphones stay with me for now.

DREW. Nice try, demon, but I think I'll be taking the headphones!

CHELSEA. No, I'LL be taking the headphones since I'm the one who bought them for him!

DREW. And, as you said, it was a sucky gift, so no takesies backsies!

FANNIE. Ohhh how I wish I could listen to Billie Holiday in high-definition.

CHELSEA. *(Even more over it.)* Okay, Ms. Evans. We get it. You're old.

FANNIE. ...Boo, you tryin' to accuse me of something?

CHELSEA. No, I'm just finding it interesting that –

FANNIE. Good, 'cause then I'd have to accuse you of bein' a plain-lookin', fetishizing, gold-diggin' trick. But since I don't think the good Lord Jesus would find that very Christian of me, I'm gonna sit here and put my dead granbaby's hundred dollar headphones in my pocket book.

CHELSEA. You can't be seri– did she really just –?? ...Davis do something!!

DAVIS. Me? Why me?!

CHELSEA. You were his best friend, and you know he wouldn't let her –

DREW. Woah woah, hold on, hey hey woah. Let's not go putting anybody in any positions, okay?

DAVIS. Thank you.

DREW. Davis was NOT Tyler's best friend alright? Childhood pal? Sure. His roommate? Yea. His gay stalker? Probably –

DAVIS. HOLD IT! Everyone just stop for TWO seconds, please! I know this is hard. I know we all want to take the right things to remember him by, and the idea of having to give up pieces of him...sucks. It sucks, and I don't want to do it any more than you do...probably even less. But...we're all here because we love him, right? We all do. So even if we don't get to take the exact thing we wanted home with us today, we can at least leave knowing it'll be in the hands of someone who loves him. Okay? Can we all just remember that?

FANNIE. *(Nodding her head to the gospel.)* Davis, sugar, yes. Yes, baby. We all just need to listen to God.

DAVIS. Yes! That! Let's do that!!

FANNIE. And His holy name is tellin' me that if this bitch leaves this house with any of my baby's things, then I am to stick this foot so far up her tiny ass, she gon' taste my slippers in her throat.

DAVIS. *(Overlapping.)* Oh my God –

CHELSEA. *(Grabs headphones.)* You want them? Your "elderly, brittle" fingers are gonna have to pry them from my hands.

DAVIS. *(Overlapping.)* Ohhhh my God –

DREW. As Tyler's PRIMARY best friend, I declare this will NOT STAND!

DAVIS. Oh my god, oh my god, oh my god...

> *(As* **CHELSEA**, **FANNIE**, *and* **DREW** *are all screaming/throwing insults/maybe hitting each other,* **DAVIS** *storms out of the room. As he does, a young Black* **WOMAN** *appears in the doorway with a jacket in her hand. She tries to interject, but everyone is too busy trying to destroy each other [with their words] to notice.* **DAVIS** *returns with a large, empty plastic container and slams it in the middle of the floor.)*

DREW. What's that?

DAVIS. It's the Charlie box!

FANNIE. Who the hell is –

DAVIS. Charlie is the little orphan boy in the homeless shelter downtown who gets all of Tyler's things I no longer want to deal with. Tyler leaves his video games on top of my bed again? Charlie box.

Tyler leaves the contents of his pockets all over the dryer again? Charlie box. Tyler DIES and isn't explicit about which incessant brat gets his stupid overpriced headphones? Charlie box Charlie box Charlie box.

SHANA. EXCUSE ME!!

> *(Everyone turns to her suddenly. She was not prepared.)*

Uh...

> *(Clears throat.)*

My name is Shana. I tried calling earlier...the door was open. Is this where Tyler Evans lives – ...used to live?

DAVIS. Wait, I recognize you from... Tyler volunteered with you, right –?

CHELSEA. What's that in your hand?

DREW. *(Almost scared.)* That's his...that's his jacket. How do you have that?

SHANA. ...Ohh. Well the police found his school ID in the pocket and Officer Jones brought it to our meeting last night. I thought I should bring it here

DAVIS. ...Oh. Well...

(Turns to others.)

Who wants it?

(And we're all uncomfortable again.)

SHANA. Uhhm...could I have that record player?

(Everyone turns again.)

See...we had this meeting a few weeks ago. And everyone was teasing Tyler for having no rhythm, 'cause well...he couldn't "walk it by himself" during the "Cupid Shuffle"...a lot of people had to walk it for him. Anyway, so he said he would prove he knew how to dance and that he had this record player with his favorite song, and he was gonna bring one of his favorite people in to sing backup for him and then we'd see how good he danced...but then he died...and then none of us were invited to the funeral. I know I wasn't. I didn't really know him though, but I knew people that knew him! But basically, point is, everyone wanted to go, and no one was invited. And I get it, we're not family. But we're still sad! And angry! So...they came up with this idea of having like a vigil that was also a march, that was also a protest, that was also a memorial celebration thing, and we could have his record player and his "favorite person" do the dance or sing the song or whatever and maybe speak on his behalf...and we would make it a big event! Like for the whole city! ...And then I guess, the police gave us this jacket. So I think the idea was I bring this jacket, you all thank me a lot, and then one of you would cry in my bosom! And then me, the person, and the record player, would go back and more or less the ending of *The Wiz* would happen… But you're not talking. And I don't feel like crying really…so…could I just have it?

(That silence.)

…Was that rude? They told me not to be rude. Oh, and to smile.

(She grits her teeth wide…it's supposed to be a smile but it's just weird.)

CHELSEA. …Tyler said he was gonna bring his favorite person with him, that night?

FANNIE. He said "favorite"? His **favorite** person?

SHANA. Well, I wasn't actually there –

DREW. So what you're saying is you came here looking for Tyler's "favorite person" to cry in your bosom and give you the record player and be the ONE person to sing and dance at this memorial slash march slash vigil?

SHANA. …I… I'm confused.

FANNIE. Give me your bosom!

CHELSEA. He was talking about me!!

DREW. I can cry the most!! Watch me!!

*(**DREW, FANNIE,** and **CHELSEA** chase **SHANA** into another room in the house.)*

DAVIS. God help me…

*(He tosses the jacket on the couch and crankily follows the others. **TYLER** enters from stage left as if he has been listening to the entire exchange.)*

Scene Four
Three Weeks Ago

(Lights shift to a warm, pleasant afternoon in the living. We happy AND cozy now. **TYLER** *observes the jacket on the couch...carefully and slowly. Then he puts it on. Just as he's starting to feel himself,* **FANNIE** *walks through the front door.)*

FANNIE. Take that rachet thing off!

TYLER. No one says "rachet" anymore, Grandmother.

FANNIE. Have they seen that jacket?

TYLER. It was a gift!

FANNIE. I said I don't want you wearin' no hoodlum's clothes. You look like a crayon box threw up on you.

TYLER. Drew has...unique taste. But besides, it's not just fashionable. It's warm, it's well-padded.

FANNIE. It's ghetto.

TYLER. Again, no one says –

FANNIE. Don't talk back to me boy. I've worked too hard for you to be trolloping around lookin' like somebody's orphan. Now take that thing off before someone picks you out of a police lineup.

TYLER. *(Sigh.)* Yes ma'am.

FANNIE. And what's all this mess on the floor? You invited me over and didn't think to clean the place up?

TYLER. Okay I'm cleaning I'm cleaning!

FANNIE. Bad enough I gotta be greeted at the front door by a pimp.

TYLER. If you keep fussin' like this I'm gonna stop inviting you over.

FANNIE. You keep talkin' to me like that, you won't have a mouth to invite no one over with.

TYLER. *(Kisses her on the cheek.)* I love you Grandma.

FANNIE. Love you too baby.

(She watches him sadly try to fold some laundry on the floor.)

FANNIE. Stop. Before you hurt yourself. Where's that little elf you keep around here? I taught him how to fold the right way.

TYLER. Davis is just getting up.

FANNIE. So is he still...?

TYLER. Gay? Yes Grandma.

FANNIE. Good. Maybe he'll knock some sense into you while you're runnin' around with them trollops.

TYLER. I'm still not sure I know what that word means.

FANNIE. It means what I said it means. A hooker? Trollop. Eddie Murphy? Trollop. That girl who keeps followin' you into my house –

TYLER. If you're talking about Chelsea...

FANNIE. I thought her name was Sarah. Or Rebecca.

TYLER. Those don't sound remotely similar. You're just being mean.

FANNIE. Or Moon. Crazy white people namin' their kids after the damn solar system.

TYLER. The point is, you gotta be nicer to her!

FANNIE. I don't gotta be nice to nobody. Fact, the only thing I "gotta" do is stay –

TYLER. "Stay Black and die." I know

FANNIE. Besides, I don't know what all there is to be huffy about. I was fine with the way things were: You go off with your little white animal cracker friends, and I sit back and make comments as I please. What's wrong with that?

TYLER. Because I would like it if you weren't tweeting hashtag shitwhitegirlssay at our wedding.

FANNIE. ...At your what-now?

TYLER. I... I'm going to ask Chelsea to marry me. For real. With a ring and everything.

FANNIE. ...Have you lost your damn mind?

TYLER. Grandma –

FANNIE. Your fifteen-year-old behind ain't old enough to be marryin' some hussy.

TYLER. Grandmother, I'm twenty-six.

FANNIE. And that makes you grown? I still wash your drawers.

TYLER. Because you won't let me!!

FANNIE. Besides, why'd you have to go and choose her? What happened to that cute little ashy girl with the afro-puffs?

TYLER. I'm not marrying my date to soph-hop.

CHELSEA. Nope, I don't like it. I don't like **her**. Choose another one.

TYLER. Why? Because she's too fun? Too smart? Too house-trained?

FANNIE. I don't need to explain myself to you, boy, you know why I don't like this.

TYLER. That's not fair! Chelsea believes in me! So much that she makes me shower every day! She makes me want to work harder for the things I want. I try harder because of her, and I'm better for it! And isn't that what everyone wants? Someone who makes you want to be even better? And I don't see why I don't get to have that just because she's white. How does that make any sense?

FANNIE. ...Child, did I do something to you?

TYLER. What do you mean?

FANNIE. I mean, what did I do to make you think you needed to be better for people?

TYLER. That isn't what I'm saying.

FANNIE. Isn't it? These people. Their schools. Their neighborhoods. Always tryin' to be better for 'em... You know I let you go to those fancy schools because you were too smart not to. Because you were as good as it gets, not so that you could be "better." Don't think I wanted to send you either...no...when you started coming home asking for money for new sneakers 'cause the kids were makin' fun of you, I knew, I KNEW, it was a bad idea. And then the ski trips, and the bar mitzvahs, and the beach houses, and the fraternities, and now you're tellin' me you wanna marry a little princess so that you can be better? Better because you're still not good enough for who, dear? For them?

TYLER. Stop saying "them"!

FANNIE. I will when they will.

TYLER. You're acting like I don't want to be Black. That's not it. I just want to be Black...and also marry who I want to marry, and go to the school that I want, and watch the TV show that I like...

(He drapes the jacket around him proudly.)

And wear a nice hoodie that makes me look a little beefier.

DAVIS. *(Entering.)* Good morning Ms. Evans.

(He kisses her quickly on the forehead, then turns to TYLER.)

Tyler, 2007 called...they want their hoodie back.

TYLER. Jesus!

(He takes the jacket off in a fluster.)

DAVIS. Am I interrupting something?

FANNIE. Tyler was just throwin' a tantrum.

DAVIS. Oh God...he didn't do the slam poem, did he?

TYLER. Don't you have somewhere to be?

DAVIS. Isn't Soulja Boy waiting for you?

TYLER. Okay, I get it. We don't like the jacket!

DAVIS. I didn't say I didn't like it. I just don't see why you have to try that hard.

TYLER. What it is that supposed to mean?

DAVIS. You know exactly what I – ...fine. Ms. Evans, Tyler has decided to devote an unreasonable amount of time to a...diverse group of college students at his alma mater. Will you please tell him he has nothing to prove to them?

FANNIE. *(Shaking her head.)* Don't do that. Don't say diverse. You know better than that.

TYLER. You tell him Grandma!!

FANNIE. And Davis, how do you feel about this Chelsea girl? I'm sure you heard about the wedding plans. Any thoughts?

TYLER. Davis LOVES Chelsea. Don't you Davis?

DAVIS. I –

TYLER. Clark Owens!

DAVIS. *(Like a robot.)* Yes. I love Chelsea. I adore Chelsea. I'd go straight for Chelsea.

TYLER. See! Davis certified! Now you HAVE to like her... Oh! I know what'll help. We have those pictures of us with baby ostriches at the zoo. There's no WAY you could say no to those.

> *(He gives* **FANNIE** *another kiss on the cheek, then exits.)*

FANNIE. Davis, sweetheart.

DAVIS. ...Yes ma'am?

FANNIE. I'm gonna ask you one more time, and don't try lyin' to me again, you understand? Do you think she's right for Tyler?

DAVIS. You...uh... You really should see those photos, they look like something out of a safari brochure –

FANNIE. Answer me. Do YOU think that girl is right for MY grandson?

DAVIS. *(Sigh.)* I don't.

FANNIE. Then we agree. There ain't gonna be a wedding. You wouldn't let him marry someone you didn't like. So what's the plan?

DAVIS. ...I'm not – ...I really shouldn't –

FANNIE. Davis.

> *(**DAVIS** takes a deep breath and then sits beside **FANNIE**. He doesn't wanna say it but...)*

DAVIS. ...I don't think she's... She's not going to say yes.

FANNIE. You don't think so?

DAVIS. I know so. Right now they're having their fun with their little banter but when it comes down to it...she wants too much for herself to settle down with him. Just let him do what he wants. He'll tire himself out, he always does. She'll say no, he'll get tired of asking, probably shave his head or go skydiving or something, and then we won't have to worry about it anymore.

FANNIE. This is why you're the one I like.

    (She stands up to leave.)

Stop poutin', honey. It ain't gonna kill the boy.

    (She exits. **DAVIS** *slumps down on the couch, head down. Very Charlie Brown. Lights suddenly go dark [not black] around him.)*

Scene Five
Present

(The apartment is scary dark and empty again. **TYLER** *enters furiously.)*

TYLER. The CHARLIE BOX?!

DAVIS. Tyler?

TYLER. You have got to be kidding me. You're sorting through my stuff, my undead, practically-horcrux-like stuff, and you brought out the Charlie box?? This is all you have to remember me by! Just this. Do you get that?! You cannot give the bits and scraps of my dying memory to some little dweeb named Charlie, who, by the way, I'm pretty sure isn't even real!!

DAVIS. Are you real?

TYLER. You are not Charlie boxing any more of my stuff. You take that stupid tub, shove it back wherever you found it, and you sit here and listen to my worshippers fight to the death over my belongings. Do you understand?

*(***DAVIS*** is like a deer in headlights.)*

DAVIS. ...Oh my God I'm losing my mind.

TYLER. And now you're freaking out.

DAVIS. It's happening. I thought I was keeping it together, too. And not like I was in denial either. Like I was actually grieving you properly.

TYLER. Davis, calm down, you're fine.

DAVIS. I was the one who called everyone, I was a rock star at your funeral. I am basically Jackie freakin' Kennedy here, and I can still see you?! You're still here?! How the hell am I supposed to – ...Is this a test? Am I supposed to burn your bones?

TYLER. No you –

DAVIS. Oh God...are you like...like HERE for me? Or no, I'm dead. I've already died. A-and this whole thing, this last week has all been my inability to let go of my time on Earth manifested in a projection of your death!

TYLER. Davis, stop! Look at me!

> *(He stands directly in front of* **DAVIS.** *They look into each other's eyes. Rapid-fire:)*

Hi –

DAVIS. Hi –

TYLER. It's me –

DAVIS. It's you –

TYLER. You're alive –

DAVIS. I'm alive –

TYLER. Yes! –

DAVIS. Are you alive? –

TYLER. No –

DAVIS. Shit!

TYLER. You can't throw all of my things out like I was never here! Because that's what everyone else out there is starting to do. They're all gonna pretend like I was never worth having here to begin with. But you know I was, right? Right?

> *(He waits for* **DAVIS** *to say "Totally!" but he doesn't...)*

...Why don't we start finding a place for these in your closet?

DAVIS. No...no...it's this stuff. This stuff needs to get out of the house! In fact...

> *(He begins furiously collecting things and throwing them in the Charlie box.)*

I'll bet Charlie would LOVE to help you find a place for your *Archie* comics.

TYLER. This isn't funny!

DAVIS. CHARLIE can have your gym socks...and CHARLIE will eat your frosted Pop-Tarts.

TYLER. Charlie did NOT earn those!

DAVIS. Oooohhhh and look at this! Charlie will looooove this.

(He holds up an American Girl doll that has clearly been beaten and worn. It's Addy!)

Sixteen YEARS I have been waiting to twist this raggedy little head around.

TYLER. YOU PUT HER DOWN! Addy did not escape from slavery to be thrown in the city streets!

(There's a loud crash and a "Shit!" coming from offstage. **TYLER** *holds onto* **DAVIS.**)

...You think that was a ghost?

DAVIS. Shut up!!

TYLER. You shut up!!

SHANA. Have you ever thought about killing someone?

DAVIS & TYLER. AHHH!!

SHANA. I did. Today. I thought about killing one of my friends. She said I couldn't be the one to come talk to you because I wasn't nice. People think because I don't smile or emote very often that I'm confrontational or something. But I can be nice. I can be friendly. I can be friendly-Black! So I didn't kill her.

TYLER. You think she's gonna kill you?

SHANA. Then I started to get into this part of town, and I looked around at the vegan coffee shops and the juice bars and I thought..."Damn, I kind of hate White people." And it's a good hate. It's deep and grounded in all the shit we've been putting up with from you all for literally centuries. But even with that, I've never even killed a White person before. Not one. Not one dead pale person.

DAVIS. I'm really uncomfortable.

TYLER. She's funny!

SHANA. Then today your friends made me sit here and tried to convince me they were allll his "favorite person" and I smiled. A lot. For four hours and twenty-eight minutes actually, I timed. I got through the bitter grandma. Sat through that chatty, vanilla fiancée. But then comes that, fratty...man-person?? And he's sitting with his legs open and offering me beer and telling me stories like I'm supposed to laugh...and all I could think was, "Bitch... If I don't kill him...someone might have to date this man. And it's going to be my fault, because I didn't kill him." But guess what?

DAVIS. You didn't kill him?

SHANA. Not even a little bit.

DAVIS. Well...I guess that means you're a good person?

SHANA. Not at all! That's the thing. Not killing people is really easy. It's the simplest shit. You just don't kill them.

DAVIS. ...Well thank you for not killing me. You know. Since you broke into my house. At two a.m.

SHANA. Oh I didn't break in. I never left! Y'all got unprotected wi-fi here and I'm outta data so... Also, I noticed Tyler's bedroom was open...and I just wanted to sit there for a little bit. I didn't know him like the others did... I remember when he started volunteering...he came a few times a week and he always tried to be... warm or some shit. Like he thought he was our big brother or something, but I didn't care. I didn't talk to him. He smiled too much... But part of me wondered what he had to be so happy about all the damn time. I found a scrapbook you left in his room... I looked at the pictures and the notes he saved and the little cutouts from Nickelodeon magazines... **He** probably never wanted to kill anyone. Right? He looked like he loved everyone...a lot of white people too. Y'all are all over that thing.

DAVIS. He didn't care about stuff like that. He wasn't –

SHANA. No I know. I know he loved his Black people too. There's a lot of family photos in it. Cousins, and uncles...but, I don't know...why aren't they here?

DAVIS. They were at the funeral...they just... I don't think he's talked to them in a while. You know...divorces... deaths in the family. People lose touch.

SHANA. So he didn't have family then...

DAVIS. Well, I was –

SHANA. Except for his grandma, right? There's not a page without her. Jesus. He would be a mama's boy...

(She tries to laugh, but kind of can't...)

So why kill him? Why do you choose to kill such a punk-ass? I wasn't there but...all you had to do was not kill him.

DAVIS. I don't really know.

SHANA. Then again, I don't own a gun. Or 400 years of White supremacy. So.

DAVIS. ...I think I'd like you to leave now.

SHANA. ...Why? What's wrong? Shit. Was I rude again?

DAVIS. Well, I don't know, you're sitting here talking to me about MY best friend's death, and...well, I'M his family. I've known him for sixteen years and you've known him for – ...You don't know him! And you said you hate white people, and I'm pretty white, but I'm grieving right now, and you're pretty not. So yeah. I'd like you to leave.

> (**SHANA** *nods, then walks to the front door. She tries to grab the handle but something won't let her.)*

SHANA. ...Are you ever afraid to walk around here at night? ...I don't think people will be expecting me around here...

DAVIS. It's not like they're gonna bother you. Just don't do anything.

SHANA. What was Tyler doing again?

DAVIS. He – ...well I wasn't –

TYLER. Yeah, I wasn't doing shit.

SHANA. Maybe you forgot...but your dead friend was Black...and he was killed. By a cop. And there's this thing that happens when you have brown skin...and you see other people with brown skin being killed by people who you were told were going to protect you... you start to feel targeted in places other people feel safe. When I read about a woman being shot in her bed, I slept on the floor for a month. And when a twelve-year-old was killed on the playground, I stopped taking my niece to the park on Fridays. Like I don't know if I'm allowed to do things anymore! So please don't tell me that I'm not grieving. I've pretty much forgotten what not grieving feels like.

(*Truth bomb. Silence.*)

...It's cold out...can I at least have his jacket? ...Since none of you want it?

TYLER. I don't think she should leave.

DAVIS. I'm not really comfortable with you taking his –

TYLER. I said I don't want her to leave!

DAVIS. You don't need to leave if you don't want to! ...You can stay upstairs –

TYLER. She can sleep in my bed!

DAVIS. Y– y-you can sleep in Tyler's bed...if you'd be comfortable with that.

(**SHANA** *turns quickly from the door as if relieved.*)

SHANA. I am... I mean... Thank you.

(*There is an awkward moment, then she begins to move toward the bedroom. She stops and turns to* **DAVIS**.)

Oh...right...also, I wanted to say that I'm very sorry... for your loss...and stuff.

(*She exits through the hallway door.* **DAVIS** *glares at* **TYLER**.)

TYLER. What? She was scared!

DAVIS. I'M scared! She wants to kill people. What's worse; she wanted to kill Drew, and then didn't! She's a tease!

TYLER. Don't talk about her like that! She's my fam– ...She's important to me!

DAVIS. Why? I don't get it! And wait a second, who the hell is this "favorite person" supposed to be?

TYLER. It's Addy.

DAVIS. Oh, shut up!!

TYLER. You shut up!! Go to sleep!

> (**DAVIS** *rolls his eyes.*)

DAVIS. ....Do you not... Do dead people not sleep or something?

TYLER. I'm not tired. Go to bed, Davis.

> (**DAVIS***' face slowly turns to concern as* **TYLER**
> *finishes sorting the Charlie box.* **DAVIS** *takes a*
> *breath, then heads offstage.*)

Scene Six
Two Weeks Ago

(DREW bursts through the front door urgently. Happy lighting. We happy again.)

DREW. I got the stuff.

TYLER. Did anyone see you?

DREW. Only the babysitter down the street, but I think I convinced him I was making a paper-mâché volcano.

TYLER. Good work, brother.

(They do a secret handshake thing.)

DREW. I have to say, the "propose to Chelsea using a fourth-grade science lesson plan" plan is your best idea yet!

TYLER. You don't need to tell me. First, Chelsea will walk through that door. "What a perfectly average day this is," she'll think

DREW. Little does she know I am but ten feet away waiting with a box of dry ice, Diet Coke, and Mentos! Damn. You're charming as hell.

TYLER. Well between you and me, I listen to a lot of Jason Mraz. I get women.

(DAVIS enters from the hallway.)

Davis! Just in time!! Drew, go start blowing up the balloons and rubbing them on your head.

DREW. On it!

(Nod to DAVIS.) Princess.

DAVIS. *(Nod back.)* Shrek.

TYLER. Davis, we need you to get into position for the proposal. Put on this lab coat, and I'll get you some latex gloves.

DAVIS. You're pro– ...

(Looks at box, then back at TYLER.)

Tyler.

TYLER. What.

DAVIS. You're getting yourself all worked up. Like with your homemade firecrackers. Or the trap you set for the Easter bunny.

TYLER. Will you be quiet? You're the best man, not Jiminy Cricket. Okay? So just help me get things together.

DAVIS. Best ma–

(Doesn't wanna say it...)

...What if she says no?

TYLER. *(Not even giving him attention.)* What are you talking about?

DAVIS. You're acting like you already have a wedding date picked out. You haven't even asked her yet. What are you gonna do if she says no?

TYLER. She's not gonna say no.

DAVIS. Right. But if she says no –

TYLER. Which she won't do –

DAVIS. How do you KNOW that??

TYLER. *(Annoyed.)* Because she's in love with me and that's what in-love people do. They say yes to being married!! Why are you being like this? What's going on?

DAVIS. *(Exasperated.)* I'm not "being like" anything. I'm just saying –

TYLER. Do you not want to be my best man?

DAVIS. That's not the point.

TYLER. Then tell me what the hell your problem is!

DAVIS. *(Pushed to the edge.)* Jesus, Tyler, she's not going to say yes!! She's going to say no! You're going to ask her to marry you, and she's going to say no. And then you're gonna stop clipping your nose hairs and you'll dry heave, and you'll start blaming Steve from *Blue's Clues* for your abandonment issues again, and I'm going to stand right here and not say I told you so. EVEN THOUGH I TOLD YOU SO! She isn't going to say yes, and you know I'm right because I'm ALWAYS right about these things. So no, I'm sorry, I don't want to be the best man at a wedding that I am positive is not going to happen! She's gonna say no to you. So grow up, wake up, and stop –

CHELSEA. *(Door bursts open.)* YES!

DAVIS. What?

TYLER. What?

CHELSEA. *(Panicked.)* Yes! I'll marry you! Like I WILL marry you – I WANT to marry you!! I want to be MARRIED to YOU! I want YOU to marry ME! You! Me! Rings! Taffeta! A Target registry!! ALL of it!

> *(She embraces* **TYLER***/kisses him on the mouth again.)*

Hold me.

> *(Their embrace is beyond happy loving yuppie couple right now.)*

TYLER. *(Glaring at* **DAVIS** *while holding* **CHELSEA***.)* ...That all sounded like a yes to me.

CHELSEA. We should celebrate. Yeah? Let's go out tonight! Well, I guess we're already going out but just – get dressed! Come on, I'll help!

> *(She pulls* **TYLER** *offstage. He flips* **DAVIS** *off as they exit.)*

> *(***SHANA** *enters just as* **CHELSEA** *and* **TYLER** *exit. Lights shift to the present.)*

Present

SHANA. Can any of them even sing?

DAVIS. Huh?

SHANA. Be honest, none of them can sing! And neither can you. He wasn't gonna bring y'all to "sing backup for him" because you can't sing!!

DAVIS. I... I don't know, I don't care!

SHANA. All we wanted was to – ...I don't know, remember him at least!! Let the world know he wasn't just some body the police left lying in the street...but apparently the only way to do that means **I** have to babysit the Animaniacs back there, hell nah, I can't do it anymore. It's making it worse!!

DREW. Shana, I just remembered, the last time we were together, Tyler spotted me for the burger I ordered. Plot twist: I have celiac's!! Which means it's probably still in my digestive system somewhere. Tyler wanted me to hold that gift inside forever, because I am indeed, his "favorite person"! BAM!

SHANA. *(To* **DAVIS** *with that "-_-" face.)* ...Bam.

(She leaves...to get her stuff.)

I'm getting my stuff.

DAVIS. Wait, Shana, I'm sorry – ugh.

(Heavy sigh/head in hands **DAVIS** *pose.)*

DREW. *(Glaring.)* ..."Quiet, mature, innocent little Davey."

DAVIS. ...Can I help you –

DREW. *(Like a private eye.)* I see right through you.

DAVIS. What?

DREW. You want us all out of the way.

DAVIS. Andrew –

DREW. **YOU** wait here for the rest of us to destroy each other, while you sit back in your little armchair... smoking cigars, and-and...stirring cauldrons!!

DAVIS. Get out of my house, Drew.

DREW. *(All up in his face again.)* I'm not in your house, temptress!! I'm in my best friend's house. I am Tyler's guest here, not yours, and if you're really so sure you're this "favorite person" well –

(He pulls out a bottle of tequila triumphantly.)

You're gonna have to drink me for it.

DAVIS. Oh my Go–

DREW. *(Ignoring* **DAVIS**, *preparing his epic speech.)* THAT'S RIGHT! An entire bottle of *Casa Dragones*!! You tried to confiscate it after bikini-casino night last year, but

I *knew* it'd find *sanctuary* in Tyler's gym bag since YOU'RE ALLERGIC TO **EX-ER-CISE**!!

DAVIS. Okay, you've made your point –

DREW. *(Growing in dramatics.)* And I alllllllllllways knew it would come to this! Well this is some violent shit right here, and Tyler drank it on two occasions; when he needed to dismantle vulnerable emotions and when he felt his masculinity was being threatened. And this, my friend, definitely falls into one of those categories!!

DAVIS. If you want to take the bottle home, that's fine, I don't care, just –

DREW. *(Now he's a villain?)* Ohhhhohohohohohoho no no NO dearest Davey. See, you and I are gonna play a little drinking game. Winner will be the one to sing Tyler's favorite song valiantly at this memorial!!

DAVIS. I don't want to sing at the stupid –

CHELSEA. *(Entering, with **FANNIE** close behind her.)* Davis it's been three days!! I keep trying to get through to that little college girl – and where the hell did she even come from?! I'M the fiancée, right? He wanted to be with me! He chose ME! A-and…of course he would want to introduce those kids to me. I'm not even trying to be competitive, this just shouldn't even be a thing –

FANNIE. You know child, I been tryin' to listen to you for the last hour, but it's hard, 'cause I can't shake the feeling that I've heard your voice on a phone sex ad somewhere.

SHANA. *(Entering and heading toward the door. She is carrying Tyler's jacket and the record player.)* You all enjoy your evening.

CHELSEA. …Why do you still have that?

SHANA. The police left the hoodie in my custody, and I figured none of you are touching it, and Tyler's dead, so, what? Do you want it?

CHELSEA. You can't have it!!

SHANA. Well who's gonna take it, then?

> *(No one responds. She puts the record player down.)*

Look, what is the deal with y'all and this jacket?

CHELSEA. It doesn't matter. You didn't –

SHANA. *(Notices the alcohol.)* Is that tequila?

DREW. We're drinking for Tyler's affection!!

DAVIS. We are NOT drinking that. Put it away.

DREW. We'll each ask questions. Get the wrong answer, you take a shot. You answer correctly, the other person takes a shot!

DAVIS. That is idiotic!

DREW. Unless of course, you already know you're not his best friend OR "favorite person," then of course, be my guest and bow out now!

CHELSEA. Drew, knock it off. It's insulting.

FANNIE. I want a shot.

SHANA. Hold on –

FANNIE. If she's gonna keep talking I wanna be drunk for it.

DREW. Ooo drunk Grandma. This will be fun!

SHANA. Can I play?

CHELSEA. I thought you were leaving –

SHANA. You said you were asking questions, right? Well I have questions.

DREW. *(Hesitates. Considers...pours that shit.)* L'chaim!

CHELSEA. You're joking.

FANNIE. We're drinking.

CHELSEA. Davis, back me up please.

DAVIS. *(Growls.)* No, Drew.

CHELSEA. Thank you.

DAVIS. Tyler drank on THREE occasions: avoiding emotion, challenged masculinity, AND to rise to performance standards! ...Sexually! ...Which never really made sense, but point is I'M GOING TO DESTROY YOU!!

DREW. *(Excitedly beginning to place down shot glasses.)* Ohohoho Davis, you've awakened a beast!!

CHELSEA. This is insane. We're not getting drunk in the middle of –

FANNIE. If you don't want to drink then just don't lose.

CHELSEA. *(Turns her head to* **FANNIE** *very slow-like.)* ...Fine. I'm not scared. I don't lose.

DREW. Okay, good, so we all understand the rules?

FANNIE. Are there any more glasses?

DREW. Uh... I don't think so, I think –

FANNIE. WRONG! The ones I gave him for his twenty-first birthday are in the cabinet. Drink up.

DREW. Wha– HEY! No! That's not fair!

DAVIS. It was a question about Tyler, and you answered it wrong. Those were your rules.

DREW. ...Fine.

> *(Pops a shot down his throat.)*

WOOO!

CHELSEA. Okay, who's next?

DREW. THAT'S A BURN!

FANNIE. Is he okay?

DREW. FEELS LIKE LEECHES ON MY INTESTINES!

DAVIS. Okay... I guess if Drew can't tell us –

DREW. Nope! Nope! I'm feelin' good. I'm in the game! Alright, Davey, answer me this: How many sports did Tyler play by the time he graduated college?

DAVIS. Seven.

DREW. WRONG! Eight. He ACTUALLY joined the bowling team for credit during fall semester of –

DAVIS. I know that. And I'm assuming you're counting the rugby team in eighth grade, but you should know he never actually played a game because he was benched the entire year. He joined eight sports teams. He only played seven of them.

> *(Pause.* **DREW** *takes another shot.)*

DREW. WOWZA! THERE IT IS!

CHELSEA. This is a waste of time.

DREW. IT'S LIKE THE TROJAN WAR IN MY UPPER CHEST!

SHANA. Here, Drew, I'll give you an easier one. You bought this jacket for Tyler, right?

DREW. Yeah. I saw it in a thrift store and I thought Tyler would like it.

SHANA. And why would Tyler like something like this?

DREW. Because we always talked about our hip-hop alter egos and I thought it made him look...you know...like notorious.

SHANA. ...Interesting. So he looked "notorious" in a jacket and now he's dead.

DREW. What are you trying to say –

CHELSEA. Hey Shana, what was Tyler's favorite TV show? Please, tell us all the little details you know about Tyler, you know, since you were such an important part of his life and all, right?

DREW. Okay, okay, no more intellectual mind games. You want to play the game, then ask questions about Tyler.

SHANA. Okay. Ms. Evans, what do you think of the jacket?

FANNIE. I thought it was cheap and ugly.

DREW. Only Tyler-questions!!

SHANA. Fine. Why did Tyler hang out with so many white people?

> (**FANNIE***'s hand shoots sky-high while everyone else is silent.*)

Nothing, boys?

DAVIS. Tyler wasn't like that.

DREW. Yeah, he didn't see us that way.

SHANA. *(Point to* **DAVIS***.)* Bullshit.
(Point to **DREW***.)* Post-racial bullshit. Ms. Evans?

FANNIE. He was in it for the HBO subscription, and the prosciutto at the country club.

SHANA. *(Nods.)* I'll drink to that.

(Takes shot.)

SHANA. Uhh excuse me, y'all didn't answer correctly.

CHELSEA. Well I didn't answer it.

DAVIS. *(Shot.)* Ohhh sweet Jesus...

CHELSEA. It wasn't even a real question. She was just being rude, and honestly, kinda – ...well, not racist, but –

SHANA. Did she just –

FANNIE. This bitch.

DREW. *(Shot, on his knees.)* HA-CHA-CHA HORNETS ARE DANCING IN MY THROAT!!

DAVIS. Are you gonna have an orgasm every time you take a shot?

DREW. What's the matter Davey, don't have any questions for anybody?

DAVIS. What did he name his stuffed lobster?

DREW. Alphie, after the frumpy attendant at the carnival dunk tank where he won it. DRINK! How old was he when he learned all the words to "Lucky" by Britney Spears?

DAVIS. Twelve. When he choreographed a dance to it with ME! DRINK! What's the one thing Tyler fears more than enclosed spaces?

DREW. The Scooby-Doo movie where the monsters are real! DRINK! February 16, 2007. Why's that date important to him?

DAVIS. It was the day *Bring It On: All or Nothing* came out on DVD. DRINK! Five things Tyler needs to survive on a deserted island.

DREW. Last one to name all five takes a double!

DAVIS & DREW. Cocoa butter.

Slim Jims.

Nail clippers.

Men's Health magazine.

And a talking animal friend!!

(Panting, out of breath, they both take shots.)

CHELSEA. Okay, slow down.

DREW. *(Panting.)* What's the matter Davey, are you scared?

DAVIS. I'm not scared, I'm just not an idiot.

SHANA. And also scared...

DREW. HA! YEAH! Up top moody Black girl!

(He raises his hand for a high five.)

SHANA. No I mean all of you. All of you are scared. Of this jacket apparently.

FANNIE. Baby, quit while you're ahead.

SHANA. You're all being weird about it. You know you're being weird about it. But I'm –

DAVIS. It's the thing that got him killed, alright?

(Another truth bomb.)

...Tyler never...he didn't wear stuff like that. The only reason a policeman would have even thought twice about him is 'cause he looked like... Ms. Evans said it herself. That jacket made him look...rough. He barely wore it out of the house until the night he – ...And Drew feels guilty for buying it for him, and Ms. Evans regrets not confiscating it...we're all blaming ourselves. So are you happy? There. That's why we're all so weird about it.

SHANA. ...Interesting.

CHELSEA. No it's not "interesting." It's devastating. We're all devastated. You really think you can come here and what? Interrogate us? When was Tyler's birthday? Hm? How about his favorite snack? Nothing? Because I thought his life mattered SO much to you.

DAVIS. Okay, I'm sorry I shouldn't have gone into it. Chels, here, why don't we just take a second and –

SHANA. No it's okay Davis.

(Takes a shot.)

I've got one for her.

CHELSEA. Forget it. I'm not playing this stupid game anymore –

SHANA. Why isn't there any blood on the jacket?

> *(She holds the jacket wide open.)*

CHELSEA. ...What are you talking about?

SHANA. When he died. Wasn't he wearing it?

CHELSEA. ...Excuse me?

SHANA. I mean you were there, right?

DAVIS. Okay, okay, we've all had a little bit to drink –

SHANA. Come on. I mean, you all think this is what got him killed, right? And you were the only one there when it happened, so I want to know. Where's all the blood?

CHELSEA. That is – ...Who the hell –

SHANA. It's not a hard question.

CHELSEA. I don't – ...I don't remember –

SHANA. Then drink.

CHELSEA. I am NOT going to –

SHANA. You don't know the answer, you drink. That's how it works.

CHELSEA. That question doesn't count.

DREW. It's not a big deal, Chels. Just take the drink.

CHELSEA. You can't honestly think I would –

FANNIE. Down the hatch baby girl.

CHELSEA. No I won't, I can't –

DAVIS. Chelsea, just take the stupid shot!

CHELSEA. I SAID I CAN'T, DAMMIT, I'M PREGNANT!

> *(She catches her breath in the silence as* **TYLER** *slowly walks into the room.)*

...Are you happy? There. I said it. I'm pregnant. With his child. So I can't drink. It's baby poison. And this is his baby. It's literally the last part of him that's still alive, and I'm not screwing that up. So... HA!

> *(She stops, catching her breath. Everyone's looking at her.)*

...Wow...okay...excuse me.

(Collecting herself.) ...Um...well I think we've all had a long night, so... Davis, maybe we should –

FANNIE. You're lyin'.

TYLER. Davis.

CHELSEA. Excuse me?

FANNIE. You heard what I said, I said you're tellin' a damn lie.

TYLER. Davis, do something.

CHELSEA. I'm not! I don't care if you don't like me. I don't care if all of you hate me. Tyler chose ME! I don't care if I have to raise this baby all by myself! I'm gonna have this piece of him with me for the rest of my –

FANNIE. Have you lost your goddamn mind, you ain't raisin' nothin'!

TYLER. I don't know what to do... Davis, tell me what I should do.

DAVIS. D-did Tyler know? Did you tell him?

CHELSEA. I swear, I was going to, that night I was going to –

FANNIE. I don't wanna hear it.

DAVIS. Ms. Evans –

FANNIE. *(Puts her hand up to him.)* I'm talking now!! You must be some piece of work to think your white ass has any business raisin' a Black baby, especially after you probably got that boy killed in the first place.

CHELSEA. You don't know what you're talking about –

FANNIE. I don't? How exactly are you gonna tell that baby what happened to its father, hm? What are you gonna do when you don't know how to brush its hair, or if its skin too dark to be that cute little biracial baby you been hopin' for? You still gonna raise it then?

CHELSEA. You're just mad because he loved me! Even despite how much you hate me, he still love–

FANNIE. *(Standing up.)* **Try raisin' your voice at me again and watch what happens!** I don't care how much he talked you up, if he bent down in front of you, if he "loved" you. You a dirty, plain, dainty trollop who wasn't good enough for my Tyler, and you ain't raisin' nothin' of his while I'm still alive.

(She walks out toward the door and grabs the tequila bottle. Takes a swig.)

Ain't no baby in my family bein' raised by you.

(She storms out.)

CHELSEA. Screw this.

SHANA. Ms. Evans, wait!

*(She chases **FANNIE** as **CHELSEA** storms upstairs.)*

DREW. …I'm like V drunk, that's what this is, right?

DAVIS. GET OUT!!

DREW. Sorry.

(He scurries away.)

*(**DAVIS**, a bit tipsy, angrily clears the shot glasses from the counter. **TYLER** watches him…then eventually leaves the room. **DAVIS** slumps down on the couch, head in his hands. Charlie Brown.)*

Two Weeks Ago, Moments After Chelsea Said "Yes"

*(Happy. **CHELSEA** walks downstairs from Tyler's room and slowly sits next to **DAVIS** on the couch. She faces forward. She wants to confide in him. **DAVIS** does not look up.)*

CHELSEA. …Davis?

DAVIS. Hm?

CHELSEA. …You know how people talk about "good guys"? …But they're usually just talking about guys who haven't murdered or assaulted anyone yet? Tyler's not a "good guy"… Tyler's like, actually good. Organic good. Right?

DAVIS. I know him, thank you.

CHELSEA. Is that why I shouldn't – ...I mean is that why you don't want me to be with him?

DAVIS. ...I just... I really didn't think you would say yes.

CHELSEA. ...Me neither.

DAVIS. Then why did you –

CHELSEA. Well...it-it's...it's complicate–

TYLER. Alright baby, let's get going.

> (*He turns to* **DAVIS** *while holding* **CHELSEA**'s *hand.*)

Davis, is there something you'd like to say to us?

DAVIS. (*No.*) ...We should probably tal–

TYLER. Really? Nothing?

> (*He turns to* **CHELSEA**.)

Chels, will you give us a minute please?

> (**CHELSEA** *nods, kisses* **TYLER** *on the cheek, gives* **DAVIS** *a half-smile, then exits through the front door.* **DAVIS** *and* **TYLER** *stare at each other.* **TYLER**'s *never been this disappointed in his friend.*)

...You know, I don't need you.

DAVIS. I get it.

TYLER. No. I'm serious. I don't need you to judge me, and I certainly don't need you to tell me what I'm not allowed to do. Because it's my life and I plan to do what I want with it.

DAVIS. No one's saying you can't.

TYLER. Oh really? "Tyler, stop spending time with people who look like you. You're MY friend so you don't get to be Black!" "Tyler, you can't marry Chelsea, she's too smart and pretty and white for you!"

DAVIS. Look –

TYLER. No. You're my friend. You help me. You support me. You don't try and hold me in some little box to make it easier on yourself. Do better. I'm leaving.

DAVIS. Tyler!

TYLER. What?!

DAVIS. Wear your stupid jacket!

> *(He tosses the hoodie forcefully from off the couch.)*

...It's cold out. You'll get sick.

> *(TYLER begrudgingly grabs the hoodie and puts it on. DAVIS sits on the couch, arms crossed, his back now to TYLER. TYLER walks toward the door, then turns around. He is about to say something, and then:)*

TYLER. ...Goodnight Davis.

DAVIS. Goodnight Tyler.

> *(TYLER turns away from DAVIS and opens the front door. He pops the hood over his head and closes the door behind him.)*

ACT TWO

Scene One
Present

(As lights come up, we hear the needle of a record player and a jazz standard plays again.* TYLER is sitting with his arms folded on the couch. His eyes begin to grow heavy as his head slowly nods over. Music stops abruptly as he quickly catches himself, jumps up, and begins pacing again.)

TYLER. NO! I'm not tired... I will not fall asleep... I'm not tired... I will not fall asleep... I will not fall asleep... I will not fall asleep... I will not –

> *(CHELSEA enters through the front door with several grocery bags and a giant, almost creepy smile.)*

CHELSEA. Oh good you're home!

TYLER. Chelsea?

CHELSEA. Well don't just stand there. Help me with the groceries.

TYLER. You can see me?

> *(CHELSEA takes her jacket off, exposing her baby bump.)*

WHAAAAT IS THAT?!

CHELSEA. What?!

---

*A license to produce *Goodnight, Tyler* does not include a performance license for any third-party or copyrighted music. Licensees should create an original composition or use music in the public domain. For further information, please see Music Use Note on page 3.

(She looks down at her bump.)

CHELSEA. Ohh don't get all squeamish now. You're the one who went on and on about how little Gonzo needed a younger sibling to go tubing with in the winter.

TYLER. ...Who?!

CHELSEA. ...Are you being weird because you forgot to take him to fencing again??

TYLER. Who is Gonzo?!

CHELSEA. I swear, you can only deprive your son of so much.

TYLER. ...We have a – ...We named our son after a Muppet?

CHELSEA. And we agreed I could name our baby girl after one of the Spice Girls.

(She kisses him and hands him the groceries.)

I got you frosted Pop-Tarts, just like you like!

TYLER. ...Dammit. I'm dreaming.

CHELSEA. No you're not.

TYLER. This feels like a dream.

CHELSEA. That's because it's my dream. I'M dreaming.

TYLER. Oh... But how did I –

CHELSEA. This is how it works. You die, and then I get to see you in my dreams. And in my dreams, we have two children named after two of the greatest musicians of our time, I'm a stay-at-home mom except I also run amazon.com from home. I'm also the mayor. And you're the CEO of a social justice law firm! How was your day at the office?

TYLER. I'm a lawyer? I'm a CEO lawyer? But I don't read!

CHELSEA. Come on!! Try it out, you'll love it!! How was your day at the office?

TYLER. It was...

(Matter of factly, as if the memories just come to him.)
...It was really busy!

CHELSEA. Yeah it was!

TYLER. And I was late for a meeting with a client to discuss synergy and budget cuts and I drank decaffeinated coffee!

CHELSEA. Yeah you did!

TYLER. And Parker tried to undermine my pocket square in front of my employees...so I FIRED him. With a glass of SCOTCH in my hand!! Hey! I LOVE your dream married life! WE RULE!!

CHELSEA. We sure do my successful entrepreneur!!

(They embrace.)

...Wait no...something's wrong...Michael Bublé should be singing right now. And where are the violas? There are supposed to be violas! Hello?!

TYLER. Don't worry about it. Michael Bublé is kind of upsetting anyway.

CHELSEA. That's not the point. We rehearsed this!! And now you're finally here, and my subconscious is trying to embarrass me?

*(**FANNIE** enters through the front door.)*

TYLER. Grandma?

CHELSEA. Oh God...no wonder...

FANNIE. You know the drill. Put on your apron!

CHELSEA. I'm going I'm going...

(She dejectedly takes off the baby bump and begins to put on an apron.)

TYLER. What's going on?

FANNIE. It's not Barbie's dream anymore. Now it's mine! How are you baby? How was school?

TYLER. School? But I thought I was the CEO of a law firm!

FANNIE. Boy, look at that hair on your head. Lookin' like a ragamuffin. Go sit by the couch so I can comb it.

TYLER. I can comb my own –

FANNIE. Sit. And take off that coat in the house.

(**TYLER** *takes off his jacket and notices he is wearing a Pokémon shirt.*)

TYLER. Why am I wearing my... I'm eight years old in your dreams?

(**FANNIE** *forces him down in front of the couch and begins to comb through his hair. At first he resists, but as she continues to comb he gets more comfortable, resting his back. This is familiar to them. Something they naturally drop into.*)

FANNIE. What'd you do in school today?

TYLER. *(Eight years old.)* ...Nuffin. I did a cool Mad Lib. Then we started talking about decimals today, but decimals are stupid and impossible so I worked on my uppercase cursive letters instead.

FANNIE. Did you bring the Tupperware back from lunch like I told you?

TYLER. Yes ma'am. Ow!!

FANNIE. Stop pullin' your head away from me.

TYLER. Well it hurts!

FANNIE. *(Wrestling with his head.)* Shhhh shhh, you're fine baby, you're fine. Stop fussin'.

(*She hums.**)

(*As she hums,* **TYLER** *calms down, eventually resting his head against her legs.*)

TYLER. This is what you dream about?

FANNIE. This is my favorite dream.

TYLER. But you could dream about anything. You could be a pirate, and I could be your parrot!

FANNIE. My dreams are very simple, sugar.

TYLER. ...Can I have a grilled cheese?

---

*A license to produce *Goodnight, Tyler* does not include a performance license for any third-party or copyrighted music. Licensees should create an original composition or use music in the public domain. For further information, please see Music Use Note on page 3.

FANNIE. Of course, baby. ALICE!

CHELSEA. *(Bitterly.)* ...Yes Ms. Evans?

FANNIE. Alice, make little Tyler a grilled cheese.

CHELSEA. Yes Ms. Evans.

TYLER. ...Why are you calling her Alice?

FANNIE. In my dreams, she's the cleaning lady from *The Brady Bunch*. Besides, I spent forty damn years in a hospital waiting on girls like her. 'Bout time one of them made you a grilled cheese.

(She continues humming.)

CHELSEA. *(Rips apron off.)* You know what? I don't deserve this! Tyler, get up! We're taking Baby Spice to our summer house!

FANNIE. *(Yanks on **TYLER**'s head.)* AH! Don't even think about it. We're staying home and braiding his hair.

TYLER. I don't like this dream.

FANNIE. Me neither! What's happening? You should be dusting my rocking chair right now.

CHELSEA. But if it's my dream you should be trapped in an endless Life Alert commercial.

TYLER. Maybe it's my dream.

CHELSEA. You're D-E-A-D. You don't get a dream.

DAVIS. *(Bursts through the front door valiantly.)* Don't worry, I'm here!!

FANNIE. I shoulda guessed...

TYLER. Davis? Where have you been?

DAVIS. Yes yes I know. I'm sorry I'm late. I got swamped with thirty million hits on my blog and advising Mark Zuckerberg and in between all my errands I had to save a little boy trapped in a well. Tyler, I got your call, what's the emergency?

FANNIE. He didn't call you.

DAVIS. Yes he did. Because he needs my help. And I always help him and then fix him, don't I Tyler?

TYLER. ...I guess in this dream you do.

DAVIS. Don't worry I know exactly what to do. Ms. Evans, you will go to the closest diner and order us all grilled cheeses. Meanwhile, Chelsea will crawl back into the John Green movie adaptation where Tyler found her. This way, no one has to fight over Tyler anymore and no relationships are threatened. Ugh! There. God bless. I fixed it.

TYLER. Wow...you DID fix it! Thanks Davis. I love you buddy!

DAVIS. And I have warm platonic feelings towards you as well, my lifelong friend.

TYLER. I don't know where I'd be without you! We should go to Olive Garden for breadsticks!

DAVIS. Oh how I wish I could. But, I gotta get ready to go. The Mr. will be here any minute to take me to the beach house where we summer.

TYLER. Jesse Williams is here?!

(**DREW** *bursts in with major Kool-Aid guy energy, but without breaking any walls.*)

DREW. Well would you look who's here! Ms. Evans, that girl from the John Green movie, and Tyler my best friend!

TYLER. ...DREW! MY **PRIMARY** BEST FRIEND!

DREW. Oohhh and there's that hot piece of Burger King!

DAVIS. Hello darling!

(**DREW** *and* **DAVIS** *embrace in a passionate mouth-kiss.*)

TYLER. ...Wait... What the hell?

DREW. Oh come on Tyler, you made peace with this ages ago.

TYLER. You married HIM?!

DAVIS. I know it seems shocking, but we had one magic night and I couldn't resist his Ultimate Frisbee musk any longer.

TYLER. ...Whose dream is this exactly?

DAVIS & DREW. I'm not saying.

DREW. Well, Tyler, buddy, ol' pal, ol' friend o' mine, we'd love to stay and chat, but we have a vacation to get to. Now, make sure to throw flowers after us as we take off. AWAY WE GO!

*(He jumps into **DAVIS**' arms ready to fly away...but:)*

...There's supposed to be a hovercraft.

DAVIS. Where the hell is our hovercraft?

*(He points to **CHELSEA**.)*

Is this John Green's doing?!

*(**SHANA** walks through the door.)*

SHANA. Hi.

*(All except **TYLER**: Groan!)*

DREW. Great. Now we get banished to the suburbs with all the other white people in Shana's dreams.

FANNIE. Joke's on you, I get to go to church choir!

(She leads happily as the unhappy white people follow close behind her, complaining.)

TYLER. Are you serious? This isn't even fair. You don't even like me that much! What? Do I have to rub your feet?

SHANA. No... I guess I just wanted to ask you a question.

*(**TYLER** sits.)*

...So, do you like...do you regret it?

TYLER. ...What do you mean? Regret what?

SHANA. I mean...working so hard? To be a good person...a person that people liked and wanted to be around.

TYLER. Why would I regret that?

SHANA. Well I don't know, obviously it didn't really pay off since you –

TYLER. Since I died. I know. Blah blah blah. "Let's all speak for Tyler the dead guy. We'll have memorials for him and make him a saint. And then we'll make news reports where he looks like a thug! Hell, we'll even dream FOR him! It'll be great!"

SHANA. ...Actually I was gonna say because you were killed. You do get that, right? You didn't just die. You were murdered.

TYLER. Of course I get that. I was there. I was the one who – of course I get that!

SHANA. I guess I would just be a little more pissed off if I were you. I mean you do all that work to be a non-threatening, well-liked, respectable Black man, and at the end of the day, they killed you anyway!

TYLER. It's not that simple.

SHANA. Isn't it? ...I don't know... I just... I'm not friendly like you were. Not a lot of people like me. I don't have very many white friends because I don't like very many white people.

TYLER. Okay, well...I'm sorry?

SHANA. I'm not.

TYLER. Oh –

SHANA. *(Defensive.)* Won't catch me shuckin' and jivin' up here so I can, what? Be like you?

TYLER. Hey, I don't –

SHANA. *(More defensive.)* 'Cause I'm nothing like you, okay? I'm like me, not like you!

TYLER. No one says you should be –

SHANA. Well good, 'cause I'm not! Don't get it twisted! Maybe the whole token-Black-friend thing works for you, but I don't come with any white yuppies attached! And it's not like I'm gonna find a man to "redeem" me or suddenly make me a happy person. I don't even wanna marry a man! I want to have a liberated lifestyle! Full of lots of detached sex! ...With lots of brown-skinned women...who are also detached! But, you know, I also want to not be killed, so then I think...I should probably smile more. And I should dress more formally. And I should start talking quieter... But YOU did some version of all of those things and you –

TYLER. I was killed anyway.

SHANA. They killed your ass anyway, so so...so it's not like being like you pays off anyway, right? Yeah. No, I don't wanna be like you, I'm-I'm **proud** that I don't live like you did.

TYLER. Then why are you here?

SHANA. ...Because I don't wanna die like you did either.

(She turns away from him, hiding her face.)

...I don't know...if it decreases my chances, or...tacks on a few extra years of being alive then...then maybe I have to give it a shot? ...But that doesn't make me like you!! Not wanting to die like you and being like you are two different things, okay??

TYLER. *(Sympathetic.)* Okay.

SHANA. *(Snap.)* Okay!

(Done. Finished. Over...but she's still standing there.)

TYLER. *(Hesitating.)* ...I'm scared too. I don't think I'm mad, but I'm –

SHANA. Afraid.

TYLER. Yeah.

SHANA. ...If – ...When I die, it's not gonna be like you. I'm not a man. It's different. People won't wanna rally behind me like they do for you... You're worried about what people are gonna remember you for...but I'm not really sure people will even remember my name...so before I sell my soul and become an Uncle Tom, I just want to know, do you regret – ...Is it worth it?

(TYLER considers it. It's too hard. He rejects it:)

TYLER. ...That's a stupid question.

(They sit in silence.)

...You know...I kind of get why they say "stay woke" now. I don't like it here. I want to wake up.

SHANA. If it makes you feel any better...you never fell asleep... I don't think dead people sleep...or dream really.

TYLER. ...We just end up in everyone else's dreams...hm...

> *(***SHANA*** slowly stands and exits out of the
> front door.* **TYLER** *starts pacing at hyperspeed.)*

I will not fall asleep I will not fall asleep I'm not tired I
will not fall asleep... I'm not tired... I'm not tired...

Scene Two
Present

> (**DAVIS** *stumbles into the room at the sight of* **TYLER** *pacing around the couch.* **DAVIS** *is clearly still drunk as hell from all of the tequila. Curiously, he begins following* **TYLER***'s footsteps and the two of them circle the couch aimlessly.)*

DAVIS. ...What are we doing?

TYLER. We're staying woke.

DAVIS. What?

TYLER. I was falling asleep. But I can't fall asleep, because if I fall asleep then I'll miss everything. I'll miss my memorial, and I'll miss your wedding, and I'll miss the birth of my child. So I'm staying awake for the rest of my li– ...I'm not going to sleep. I'm staying woke.

DAVIS. Okay.

> *(He stumbles and falls on the couch. After a moment of confusion:)*

...LET'S GO DANCING!

TYLER. What's wrong with you? Why aren't you reprimanding me?

DAVIS. Let's just GO! Just like we used to. We'll just – ...just like – drive somewhere far, like to some CRAZY city, like...like "Jersey City" or something, and we'll just like dance our asses off...like COMPLETELY!

TYLER. How much tequila did you have?

DAVIS. WAIT! ...Can you FLY?! You're a ghost right?! You can like...you can like fly and shit, right?!

TYLER. You're drunk.

DAVIS. You're ugly. Let's fly to Tulsa.

TYLER. I can't fly, Davis.

DAVIS. *(Childlike mocking.)* "I can't fly, Davis."

TYLER. We don't have time to play around right now, okay?!

DAVIS. ...Okay.

TYLER. Good –

DAVIS. Yeah it's cool, it's chill.

TYLER. Thanks –

> (**DAVIS** *jumps on to the couch, holding the
> tequila bottle like a microphone.*)

DAVIS.

MIIIIIISSSSS –

TYLER. Da–

DAVIS. *(Jumping on the couch, doesn't stop for* **TYLER.***)*

SUZY HAD A STEAMBOAT, THE STEAMBOAT HAD A BELL

TYLER. Please don't.

DAVIS. *(Simultaneously.)*

TOOT-TOOT! THE STEAMBOAT WENT TO HEAVEN, MISS
SUZY WENT TO –

TYLER. Stop –

DAVIS. *(Prancing around the room.)*

HELLO OPERATOORR, PLEASE GIVE ME NUMBER NINE,
AND IF YOU DISCONNECT ME I WILL CHOP OFF YOUR
BE**HIND** THE FRIDGERATOR, THERE WAS A PIECE
OF GLASS, MISS SUZY SAT UPON IT, AND BROKE HER
LITTLE –

(Placing tequila bottle in **TYLER***'s face.)* Come on come
on come on, broke her littlllleeeeee...

> (**TYLER** *sighs exasperatedly and turns away
> from* **DAVIS***...until he can't help but leap onto
> the couch and join in.*)

DAVIS & TYLER. *(Hyping each other up in their favorite
childhood rhyme.)*

ASK ME NO MORE QUESTIONS, TELL ME NO MORE LIES,
THE BOYS ARE IN THE BATHROOM, PULLING DOWN
THEIR **FLIES** ARE IN THE MEADOW, THE BEES ARE
IN THE PARK, MISS SUZY AND HER BOYFRIEND ARE
KISSING IN THE **D-A-R-K D-A-R-K DARK! DARK! DARK**
IS LIKE A MOVIE, A MOVIE'S LIKE A SHOW, A SHOW IS
LIKE A TV SHOW AND THAT IS ALL I KNOW! MY MA

GAVE ME A NICKLE, MY PA GAVE ME A DIME, MY SISTER GAVE ME A BOYFRIEND, HIS NAME IS FRANKENSTEIN! HE MADE ME WASH THE DISHES, HE MADE ME SCRUB THE FLOOR, AND WHEN HE ASKED TO MARRY ME I KICKED HIM OUT THE DOOOOOOOORRRRRR

(Having totally exhausted themselves, they fall onto the couch in laughter. They're lost in that "and ohhh how they laughed" kinda moment with each other, almost in tears.)

DAVIS. What about the forty-acre bra part though?

TYLER. Grandma said we can't sing that part anymore.

DAVIS. Fair.

*(He lovingly lays on **TYLER**'s lap.)*

Man I was so in love with you.

TYLER. ...What?

DAVIS. I know that's why you're here. Why I keep seeing you all the time, and no one else does. It's 'cause I used to be in love with you and I never told you.

TYLER. Davis –

DAVIS. And it was for a really long ass time. For pretty much three quarters of our friendship I was just waiting for the right moment to...but I never did. Because you don't love me back, right?

TYLER. Of course I do.

DAVIS. Well, yeah, duh, you love me. But not *that way*, right? You can say it. It's fine.

TYLER. No... I guess not like that, no.

DAVIS. Right! And I realized that years and years ago. In twelfth grade when you went to prom with that sophomore even though I thought we were gonna go alone...you know, but like...together...I got over you! And then three years later, I realized I wasn't...and then you got in your first real, grown-up relationship and we had to stop cuddling so much. So I sucked it up...and I got over you. And then when I realized I still wasn't, and we graduated and you went on a gap year to Israel, and I got an unpaid internship, I got over you. Over and over, I had to keep getting over you. And I did it. Every single time because...well, you're my best friend...you're like...the love of my life basically. And being IN love with you was ruining that. So then last year you asked to move in with me...and despite my better judgment...I said yes. And one morning I looked at you eating your cereal, with your eye boogers...and I was like..."He looks a little bit like Martin Lawrence"... and also you're a little bit of a dweeb... Actually, you're a total dweeb and I laughed because...that's SO not what I want. I want...a ruggedly sexy, charming, chiseled young college professor named...Brogen! And I want him to see me and to love me **"that way."** He'll want to hold me, and kiss me on the mouth, and when I take him home it'll be to a house that you don't live in. We will have sex on a counter that you didn't eat your frosted Cheerios on every morning, and we'll sleep in a bed that your dirty clothes have never been sorted on. And it's not because I don't love you...like I said, "love of my life"...but my life can't be all you. It can't. And if looking at you and telling you this is what I have to do to really let go of you...then okay.

(*Deep sigh and smile.*)

I loved you. I love you. And I am so...over you. And, now...you can go.

(*Silence.*)

I really mean it Tyler. It's okay for you to go. You don't have to haunt me anymore.

(**TYLER** *walks up to* **DAVIS** *and looks deeply into his eyes.*)

TYLER. ...Davis, I'm only going to say this to you one last time.

DAVIS. Yes?

TYLER. This is not. about. you.

DAVIS. ...Not about me?

TYLER. I'm the one who –

DAVIS. Not about ME?!

TYLER. Davis!

DAVIS. *(Rage.)* How DARE you?! You are in MY living room. Your family is drinking tequila in MY house. You are haunting ME! I haven't had a SECOND alone since the night that you died dealing with all of your shit, and you're going to tell me it's not about ME?! All I wanted was to grieve you. Maybe cry over your casket or collapse over an old sweater or something. But no. Because you died in public, and Black, and important so I've lost the right! Instead of getting hit by a car, or getting cancer or something normal, you had to go and die a monument, so now I have to –

TYLER. *(Black rage!)* I DIDN'T ASK TO BE ANYONE'S DAMN MONUMENT!!

 (Silence.)

I was told that in life I only had to do two things. Stay Black and die. That was it. And I did both. So in return, I would have liked two things, AT LEAST two: a decent-looking obituary photo and to name my own child. But now? I didn't even get an obituary. There is a picture in the newspaper of my body lying in the middle of the street. My face isn't even in it! My TWICE as handsome as Martin Lawrence's face-FACE! So out of the two things I asked for, I'm getting neither! I'm not getting to name my own child, Davis, and I did what I was supposed to do. I held up my end of the bargain. I stayed Black and then I died...do you hear that? Do you hear it when I say it now? I'm dead. I died. I ACTUALLY died!! I should be angry, I should be pissed off, I should be – I should be SOMETHING but I'm just dead. I'm DEAD. I'M dead, and you – you-you get to stay here. You get to stay here and grow and make new friends, well **I** deserve that too. I deserve all of that and – and MORE. MORE. I actually deserve it MORE than you –

DAVIS. Okay, stop it.

TYLER. I was nicer than you! I was a better friend than you are!! I-I...I would NEVER make you feel stupid for wanting to marry the person you love, I would NEVER. I did everything right but YOU acted like a selfish ASSHOLE.

DAVIS. Stop it, why are you being so –

TYLER. You get to be a selfish asshole and you STILL get to be alive?? Why?? Because you're – because – because you're white? You're my brother. You're my best friend... you're...you are the love of **my** life. And...and you get to have what I can't. You get to be whoever you want! And there has – there HAS to be some reason that I – ...

(He catches his breath.)

...There are people who want to gather and protest in my name. There are mothers, and fathers, and children who heard the story of what happened to me...and... maybe they'll make graphic tees with my face on it, or I'll inspire a revolution or something. I don't know. But I would have traded all of that in a SECOND for the – ...I just want to name my child. That's all.

(He takes a deep breath and sits on the couch.)

I didn't ask to be a monument. But dammit if not being shot was too much to ask, then hell, I guess I'll take it.

DAVIS. ...I want you to leave.

TYLER. Shut up.

DAVIS. I'm serious. I don't want you here anymore. I don't care how much I'll miss you. This is ten times worse. So go! Please God, go! Go die, actually.

TYLER. FINE! You want to me to go? I'll go! I'll die right now. Watch me!

DAVIS. Then do it! Go!

TYLER. Oh I WILL! And you think I'll miss it here? I won't. I don't give a damn about being alive. I'm not gonna miss your racism, a-and, and your "breathing"!

DAVIS. And I won't miss your funky-smelling breath either.

TYLER. Oh what? You think being alive is so great?! Well guess what, I'm going to heaven! So HA! Joke's on you. You'll be down here struggling to pay bills, and I'll be up there; playing Mancala with Jesus and Luther Vandross!!

DAVIS. GOOD FOR YOU! AND IF YOU SEE MY AUNT NANCY UP THERE, HAVE FUN! WE DON'T NEED YOUR TOE FUNGUSES!

TYLER. WHATEVER! THERE AREN'T ANY *FUNGI* IN HEAVEN.

(He walks out of the front door.)

I'M GOIIIING!!

DAVIS. GOOD RIDDANCE!

TYLER. HERE I GO. OFF TO HEAVEN!!

DAVIS. BYE!!

TYLER. "OH HEY GOD! ARE THOSE GUMMY WORMS FOR ME?? NO WAY, AMY WINEHOUSE. THEY LET YOU IN?!"

DAVIS. GIVE THEM TEN MINUTES! THEY'LL HEAR YOUR CHIPMUNK IMPRESSION AND SEND YOU STRAIGHT DOWN TO HELL!!

(No response.)

WHAT? NOTHING TO SAY?!

(No response.)

...Tyler?

(He sits for a moment, then hops up in a panic, running to the door.)

Tyler wait –

(He's gone...)

TYLER. *(Walking in from hallway door on some ghost-y shit.)* I'm still here.

*(**DAVIS** takes one of the couch pillows and furiously hits **TYLER** upside the head with it.)*

DAVIS. DON'T DO THAT!

TYLER. Stop whining.

DAVIS. God, you're such an asshole. If you're gonna go, then go! Don't keep leaving, or saying you're gone...a-and... and being here anyway. It's too much. It's too –

TYLER. Where am I supposed to go? Tell me!

DAVIS. Away from ME! Aren't there other people you can bother? Bother Shana!! Since her and her little friends are all SO important to you now, haunt her!!

TYLER. That's not fair. Why won't you lay off of that?

DAVIS. Because you keep trying to shut me out of your life! You wanna get married, and then you want to spend more time with these kids I can't relate to and make fun of me for not being like you guys or whatever –

TYLER. It had nothing to do with you, Davis, I just don't have a very big family, okay?!

(Beat.)

I barely remember my mom...I haven't talked to most of my cousins since I was nine...it's always just been me and Grandma and – ...I just wanted to remember what it felt like to be around a lot of people who were...like me. It doesn't mean I don't love you! I just...like God, am I not allowed to have both? Jeez.

> (**DAVIS** *sits down beside him. Both sit in silence for a moment.*)

DAVIS. *(Doesn't want to ask.)* ...How did it happen?

TYLER. What?

DAVIS. Why did he... Why would someone hurt you? I mean, what did you – ...What happened? I'm asking. I'm really asking.

TYLER. Oh...okay...uhh...

Scene Three

(A light raises upstage left, revealing **CHELSEA** *sitting on a chair. It is unclear to us where she is or who she is speaking to, but it's clear that she is separate from* **TYLER** *and* **DAVIS**. *Lights go down on everything except for* **CHELSEA** *and* **TYLER**, *who are facing out, telling the story.)*

TYLER. So after we left the house, we went out to celebrate. It was our anniversary.

DAVIS. No it wasn't –

CHELSEA. I really like anniversaries. Tyler used to make fun of me for keeping track of all our firsts in my calendar.

TYLER. Remember the beagle calendar? I only bought it so I could fill it up with anniversaries for us to celebrate. You know like first fights.

CHELSEA. First "I love yous."

TYLER. First sleepovers!

CHELSEA. First brunch!

TYLER. First drunk-brunch.

CHELSEA. Last drunk-brunch which was the same as the first drunk-brunch.

TYLER. So this week we celebrated by going to our favorite karaoke bar. It was our karaok-a-versary.

CHELSEA. It was our "first kiss" anniversay...so I thought we were going to the bar where my ex-boyfriend broke Tyler's nose...but, I guess I was distracted.

TYLER. She was acting sort of strange.

CHELSEA. I wasn't ready to tell him. About the baby. I didn't want him to think that's why I said yes –

TYLER. So I figure it has something to do with wedding jitters! So I tell her we should forget the bus –

CHELSEA. The bus never shows up.

TYLER. And now I can show her how I'm gonna "zig-a-zig-AH!" down the aisle since we gotta walk anyway.

CHELSEA. Tyler starts walking like he has something stuck up his butt, so I'm not totally sure what was happening to be honest.

TYLER. I think I intimidated her.

CHELSEA. But I know he's trying to get me to laugh. And I do. I always do. But like –

TYLER. It was raining.

CHELSEA. NOW it's pouring and I'm soaked, and he's – ... still smiling. But I'm shivering!

TYLER. I could see that ma' lady was a little chilly, so I bust out some of that good ol' chivalry and –

CHELSEA. He takes off that God-awful hoodie and puts it on my head.

TYLER. I get women.

CHELSEA. I try to go left, but he tries to go right –

TYLER. She wants to go north, but we're supposed to go south –

CHELSEA. Which is south, but we need to go north, 'cause Sam's is up north.

TYLER. And right is south, so left is wrong, and I am right!

CHELSEA. I pull out my phone to prove him wrong.

TYLER. Her phone can't help 'cause it's getting wet again and I keep trying to tell her to get a damn case for it but of course –

TYLER.	**CHELSEA.**
She lives a reckless lifestyle.	I live a reckless lifestyle.

TYLER. So we finally go my way because she trusts my intellect.

CHELSEA. Because he whines.

TYLER. And we're finally there! I try and get us a seat at the bar because one time we spun on these bar stools for like three hours until Chelsea had too much to drink.

CHELSEA. I didn't recognize the place until I remembered we spun on the bar stools once until Tyler puked on the bartender... And then he goes –

CHELSEA & TYLER. HAPPY KARAOK-A-VERSARY!!

TYLER. ...And she just leaves.

CHELSEA. I know it sounds dramatic but it wasn't even the anniversa– ...All I kept thinking the entire way there was "you're making excuses you're making excuses." It felt like my excuse. Having a baby felt like an excuse to say what I wanted to say all along which was... which was what I said. "Yes." ...But that's messed up, right? My baby can't be an excuse for something, that's disgusting, and just – between the rain, and the iPhone, and the wrong anniversary, and that-that STUPID jacket... I just left. Without saying a word to him.

TYLER. I take off after her. Without thinking.

CHELSEA. He's following me, and he's calling my name over and over –

TYLER. Maybe I was too loud.

CHELSEA. We get to the corner and he touches my back.

TYLER. Maybe I was too close to her.

CHELSEA. And I just shout, "DON'T TOUCH ME" at the top of my lungs.

TYLER. *(A hiccup. Takes a second.)* ...There was an officer there. Across the street. And he was really hype about something. He starts screaming at me...and I guess I realized how it might have looked... I'm...bi-bigger than Chelsea so I realize I should try to explain.

CHELSEA. I saw Tyler's face first. I didn't even know the officer was there until...he was yelling something at Tyler, asking for his name again and again...and Tyler keeps saying, "This is my girl! This is my girlfriend!"

TYLER. "This is my girlfriend, this is my fiancée, I promise."

CHELSEA. I didn't move.

TYLER. He wouldn't believe me. I tried, but he was getting louder so I remembered what Grandma told me.

CHELSEA. And he's patting his jeans and looking for something and I don't know what's happening...until I realize I'm still wearing the jacket.

TYLER. I look for my college ID.

CHELSEA. And his wallet's in the pocket –

TYLER. I think I turned to Chelsea then –

CHELSEA. I think he wanted me to give it to him –

TYLER. But I can't really remember this part –

CHELSEA. The officer must have seen him touch me because he –

TYLER. I just heard something –

CHELSEA. Because he shot him.

TYLER. I think I fell –

CHELSEA. He just shot him down two feet in front of me, a-and-and –

TYLER. The rain was loud –

CHELSEA. And-and I still have the jacket on –

TYLER. The rain was lou–

CHELSEA. Tyler falls-he-he falls two feet in front of m–

TYLER. I think Chelsea was screaming, I think maybe I screamed –

CHELSEA. I drop my phone, and I have his jacket on –

TYLER. But the rain was really really lou–

CHELSEA. And it's my fault because I had his jacket on-I had his jacket on! If I had just...taken the jacket off faster, if he had the jacket –

TYLER. If I hadn't said anything, or-or if I hadn't been so close to her –

CHELSEA. Or-or if I had just stayed closer to him so he didn't cross the street-or –

TYLER. If-if we had taken the bus like we were supposed to –

CHELSEA. If I hadn't made such a big deal about the calendar –

TYLER. I should've had my ID in my back pocket like I always do –

CHELSEA. I left the restaurant –

TYLER. I should've been still –

CHELSEA. I ran down the street –

TYLER. I should've put my hands up higher –

CHELSEA. *(Words getting away from her as her panic/speed increase.)* I should have broken up with Jake earlier, because then there'd be no one to punch Tyler when he kissed me at my staff Christmas party – Or I should have kept my mouth shut instead of asking for his help carrying my groceries home that day, b-b-because most likely, probably, if he never met, if he wasn't on that street next to me, trying to get me to listen, he would be alive right now and –

SHANA. Chelsea, stop!!

> *(Lights rise around* **CHELSEA** *to reveal* **SHANA** *and* **FANNIE** *sitting on either side of her. Back in the sad living room.* **TYLER** *is gone.* **FANNIE** *sits with her back to both* **SHANA** *and* **CHELSEA***.)*

...That's enough.

CHELSEA. *(Struggling to get her breath.)* ...I'm sorry... I didn't mean to –

SHANA. It's fine, you don't need to – ...We don't need to hear any more.

> *(Takes a deep breath.)*

I know this is hard...but I wanted to talk to both of you because...we'd still really like it if all of Tyler's family could be at the memorial tomorrow. I think Tyler would want you to stand for him together, and it would really mean a lot to me – ...Is there any way you can... I don't know, figure something out and stand with each other?

CHELSEA. ...Ms. Evans... I know how awful you must think I am. I do. Keeping the baby a secret all this time... I know how manipulative and selfish it must all seem –

SHANA. If we could –

CHELSEA. And-of-of course, of course you all loved him so much, and there's no way I could compete with that, there's no way –

SHANA. Chelsea –

CHELSEA. Please! ...I just need to finish, please.

(Deep breath as **SHANA** *backs off.)*

...I didn't think I was good enough...to be a part of this family. But – ...but HE thought I was a-and...and this baby, it just sort of felt like a...like a sign...

(She turns to **FANNIE.***)*

...I know you think this is my fault. I know if he wasn't with me he would...he would probably be alive right now –

SHANA. NAH! If a police officer **hadn't SHOT him** he would still be alive right now. I'm sorry...I'm not trying to be mean, but this...blaming and fighting and basic pettiness coming from all of you, it's useless!! To me and everyone like me. It's 'cause of shit like this that I gotta be up here, holdin' your hand and collecting the boy's gym socks in the first place.

CHELSEA. If I'm such a nightmare then why are you still talking to us!

SHANA. 'Cause if it takes a buncha baby pictures and spelling bee trophies for people to actually care when one of us gets shot, then I guess I don't have much of a choice, do I?

CHELSEA. Of course you have a choice! That's the difference. You don't have to be here because you didn't lose anyone, not like we did, you weren't there! I was there, I saw him –

SHANA. And you're sitting here yelling at me like I ain't next!! Like I'm not sitting here with a big ol' bullseye on my forehead, well I'm sick of it. You all thought that Tyler was killed because he looked "dangerous" in a jacket. YOU were wearing the jacket. They shot him because he was Black. End of story. So we're giving him his parade, because when I go, I want mine too. Mothers are trying to dress their sons so they survive the walk to school! Little Black girls braiding, twisting, perming, like a hairstyle will decide if they come back home alive that day.

As IF any of that even matters. As if the problems are the choices that WE'RE making. You and Davis and Drew...you all loved him...you love him, but every moment you spend making this about yourselves, you are distracting from the whole damn system that doesn't want us alive, making ANY choices in the first place.

(Packing her stuff.) I'm getting my parade! I don't care what stock user-friendly-bitch's face gotta be on my poster, someone's gonna give a damn when I die!!

(She angrily turns to **FANNIE**.*)*

Why aren't you saying anything?

(No response.)

Ms. Evans, I need you to speak! I don't get why you don't have more to say. You're sad and annoyed and that's fine, but you have to be angry too, right? Aren't you angry? Be angry!

*(***FANNIE*** *slowly looks up at* ***SHANA***/puts the fear of God in her with just a look.)*

FANNIE. ...You don't talk to me like that.

SHANA. You aren't –

FANNIE. You don't EVER talk to me like that.

SHANA. I wasn't trying to –

FANNIE. Smart-ass little college girl, thinkin' she can walk up in here and tell me how to talk. I don't know who raised you to think like that, but you seem confused, baby, so I'm gonna remind you: We are not equals. I am not your friend. I am not your peer. You do not get to lose your temper with me. I have worked too hard for too long, and you haven't even started. So you will not talk to me like I am some fool who don't know any better, and if you forget it again, I promise I will smack it back into you, little negro, do you understand me?

SHANA. ...Yes ma'am.

CHELSEA. ...Ms. Evans –

FANNIE. And you. What? Were you afraid I forgot about you? Because I have to be honest, sugar, I'm not sure why you're still here.

CHELSEA. All I did was – ...I just loved him. All we did was love each other, and you're mad, why? Because I have white skin, and what else?

FANNIE. That would be enough of a reason.

CHELSEA. ...Fine. Well I wish it didn't take so little for you to hate me.

FANNIE. Don't even try it. Please, I don't "hate" you because you're white. If I hated you it'd be because you're spoiled, and entitled, and downright disrespectful. But I don't. I don't got the energy for it. If I hated everyone I should for being white the exhaustion woulda done killed me a long time ago.

CHELSEA. ...You don't have to like me! I just – I don't understand why you couldn't have let him –

FANNIE. ...Because you were not safe for him. You...those boys...he loved you with everything he had and – none of y'all were safe for him. You never have been. And if you don't believe me, ask that man why he reached for his gun when he saw a Black man standing next to a small white woman in the street.

CHELSEA. I can't keep – GOD – I don't know how to apologize to you, Ms. Evans, he left me too!!

FANNIE. (*'Bout ta smack the shit out of this girl.*) HE DIDN'T LEAVE YOU! HE DIDN'T LEAVE. HE WAS TAKEN! Somebody took him from ME, to protect YOU. Your people. They out here killin' us thinkin' they're helping you. THAT is why I won't hug you. THAT is why I will not wipe your tears, because that ain't gonna do shit to help any of us.

(**CHELSEA** *breaks out in tears.*)

Ohhh you poor child. You think you're a part of this because you "loved" him? ...I raised the boy! Everything about him you adore, that made you smile and laugh, I built from scratch! You love what I made.

But me? I loved him before he could bathe himself, or even knew how to open his eyes. I loved him when his mama couldn't. Then she died. She left. But I still loved him. I still stitched him together piece by piece 'til he was ready to go out in the world and be loved by other people. You think you know what it is to love him, but that's only possible because I did it first.

(She begins to drift into her own a bit.)

...He was only two years old when his mama died. Never knew his father...hell, I never knew his father. But after she was gone...Tyler wouldn't sleep for nights. He cried and fussed, I couldn't get him to sit still... finally I got tired myself and played an old record to keep me from losin' my own mind. I wasn't even tryin' to put him asleep 'til I looked over and noticed he was knocked out there on the floor...seemed to do the trick, so I started playing it for him every night and every night it worked like magic. I sang him to sleep every single night until he was seven years old.

(She sits in silence, then slowly, softly, begins humming to the same jazz song we've heard a few times now. Eyes closed and swaying, she *gets lost in it for a moment...then opens her eyes again, disappointed.)*

...There's nothing left to say. He's gone. And it's just me, left behind, again...

(The three sit in silence. **CHELSEA***'s head is down.)*

CHELSEA. ...I wish I hadn't said it. "Don't touch me." Even if that wasn't the reason he – ...Either way...that'll be the last thing I ever said to him...

(Looking to **FANNIE***.)* ...He made me better. You said you made him, well...what you made...made me want

---

*A license to produce *Goodnight, Tyler* does not include a performance license for any third-party or copyrighted music. Licensees should create an original composition or use music in the public domain. For further information, please see Music Use Note on page 3.

to be a better person. And I don't know how to do that...without him here.

FANNIE. *(After some silence.)* Young lady, look at me.

> (**CHELSEA** *looks.*)

You want to be a better person? Stop crying and be better.

CHELSEA. I don't –

FANNIE. Stop crying. Right now.

CHELSEA. You don't... You don't want me to be sad? You don't want me to –

FANNIE. Not in front of me.

CHELSEA. ...Yes... I –

> *(She stops.)*

Yes ma'am. I understand.

> *(She stands and wipes her face with her hands.)*

(To **SHANA.***)* I'll be there tomorrow. Thank you.

> *(She grabs her things and exits, leaving* **SHANA** *and* **FANNIE** *to sit in silence.)*

FANNIE. Nothing to say?

> *(No response.)*

Answer me when I'm talking to you. Why you so quiet all of a sudden?

SHANA. ...I'm tired.

FANNIE. *(Sigh.)* Me too.

SHANA. ...But we can't stop yet...can we...

FANNIE. Like I said. I will when they will.

> *(She holds out her hand.)*

Come on.

> (**SHANA** *considers the hand for a moment, then grabs it. She helps* **FANNIE** *to her feet. They exit the house together.)*

Scene Four
Three Months Ago

(TYLER and DREW are on the couch in the dark, the light of the TV on their faces. TYLER is clutching his American Girl doll, Addy, to his chest. He and DREW are sitting on opposite sides of the couch, a look of discomfort on both of their faces as they watch the screen intently.)

DREW. ...Are you scared? –

TYLER. No!

(He waits.)

...Are you scared? –

DREW. Of course not. Why would I be scared??

TYLER. Right! I mean, everyone knows the monsters aren't real. Any minute now Fred is gonna make a trap that Scooby and Shaggy will ruin by running headfirst into a conveniently placed bookcase, and the zombie will end up being a disgruntled, bitter, sexually frustrated security guard.

DREW. Yup...all thirty-seven zombies.

(He waits.)

...Have you ever seen this movie before?

TYLER. No.

DREW. You should probably keep holding Addy.

TYLER. I told you I'm not scared!

DREW. I'm not scared either I'm just glad you have Addy. You know, for the company.

TYLER. Fake zombies aren't scary! White people with cornrows, now that's scary!

DREW. Right! But this? NOT scary. We're men!

TYLER. Exactly! ...But don't tell Davis we watched this.

DREW. Why not?

TYLER. We watched *Goosebumps* last Halloween and I slept at the foot of his bed for three weeks. So now I'm not allowed to watch horror movies.

DREW. Ugh. Why does Davis have to be such a mom all the time?

TYLER. He's not a mom. He's just protective.

DREW. He checks if your toothbrush is wet at night to see if you've brushed your teeth.

TYLER. ...Okay, fine, he's a little bit of a mom. But that's only because he cares about me. I mean, that's the kind of mom I would want to be.

DREW. Not me. When I have kids, I'm gonna let them watch whatever they want. I'm not gonna be mean, or make them drink milk or yell at the – TYLER COVER YOUR EARS AND SHUT YOUR EYES!

TYLER. DID SCOOBY DIE?!

DREW. JUST KEEP THEM SHUT!!

(Watching intently.) ...Uhhh... I think...yeah...yeah I think the zombies are definitely real.

TYLER. Oh God...

DREW. Should I put the game on?

TYLER. NO! We are MEN! We don't need to hide behind Football. We can finish a damn Scooby-Doo movie! ... Just tell me when I can open my eyes.

DREW. Okay...

TYLER. ...I am SO not letting Tyson watch this shit. This is horrible.

DREW. Who's Tyson?

TYLER. It's Tyler and son put together. When Chelsea and I get married we're gonna have a son named Tyson... And if it's a girl; Tyla. And if it's a cat, Tyger.

DREW. You think about that sort of stuff?

TYLER. Of course I do.

DREW. And THAT doesn't scare you? I mean asking a woman to marry you?! ...And – and...and having a little human thing that you have to keep alive?

TYLER. I actually kind of want two little human things. That way they'll compete for our attention, and the chances of them being Olympic athletes is a lot greater.

DREW. Huh...

TYLER. Besides, I don't see what there is to be afraid of about marriage. I mean, the worst she could say is no... and if she does that...well...I do something else. I mean, I'll listen to angrier music and weep a little bit, but if she doesn't want to marry me then my dream doesn't work anyway. And I'm not scared of that.

DREW. I guess I get that. So two kids?

TYLER. And a hypoallergenic puppy. And you'll be their godfather.

DREW. I will? ...Davis won't?

TYLER. Davis will be their godfather too!

DREW. Oh.

TYLER. I mean if you can have two moms or two dads, then you can have two godfathers.

DREW. Are you saying we're gonna be two gay dads?

TYLER. I just want them to have both of you. And my grandma. And my hairline. It's my family and that's the way it goes.

DREW. That's fair I guess...but can I be the one to teach them how to eat Oreos?

TYLER. Oh of course. Can I open my eyes yet?

DREW. Not until it's safe! ...See? I can be a mom too!

TYLER. You're such a bro. I love you.

(**DAVIS** *walks in from the hallway.*)

DAVIS. Why's it so dark?

DREW & TYLER. *(Bloody murder.)* AAAAHHH!!

DAVIS. WHAT IS WRONG WITH –

(*He notices the TV.*)

...Tyler!! What did I tell you about watching this crap?

TYLER. Drew made me.

DREW. I did not! We're being brave!

DAVIS. Did Tyler tell you what happened last time he tried to be brave with a cartoon horror film?

DREW. He sure did! And now we're conditioning. Okay? Sit!

DAVIS. Fine.

>*(He sits beside* **TYLER.***)*

...Why do the zombies look like that? ...Aren't they supposed to be – ...They're fake right?

TYLER & DREW. Are you scared?

DAVIS. NO.

>*(He waits.)*

...Tyler, please go get my Beanie Babies.

TYLER. I got you, buddy.

>*(He jumps up and exits through the hallway, leaving Addy between* **DREW** *and* **DAVIS.** *There is some silence. The lights rise, and the look of fear on their faces becomes a more tired look mixed with discomfort.)*

Present

DAVIS. They'll be here soon to pick us up...

DREW. Okay...hey Davis.

DAVIS. Hm?

DREW. ...I'm scared.

DAVIS. ...Of what?

DREW. I don't know... I mean...do you miss him?

DAVIS. Well –

DREW. Of course you miss him. Sorry, that was dumb. I just meant... I know everyone's really sad, and upset. Death is really sad. He was my best friend, and he died, and that's enough to be depressed about...but on top of that... I just miss him. I miss hearing him laugh at my dumb jokes...and I miss watching dumb shit on TV with him. Every day there are these things I want to do...and I usually did things with him, but now I can't do that anymore...and now I'm scared because...what if it's like that all the time now? Like, I used to really like eating cheesesteaks before, but now it just makes me think of every time we ate cheesesteaks, and then I can't eat it. And Tyler taught me how to bench press, so I don't know if I can ever go to the gym again. I mean... I wanna do things...but all of it just reminds me that I'm never gonna see him again...and so... I'm scared of doing a lot of things now.

DAVIS. ...Did you ever do things with other people?

DREW. ...Not a lot. To be honest, I think I annoy people sometimes.

DAVIS. That's true...but I don't know...we all wanted a lot from him...maybe you should do things with other people who miss him that much. Like Ms. Evans! ...I don't think she likes us very much...but I don't want her to get lonely. Tyler wouldn't want us to leave her alone, so even though she'll probably make you clean a lot, it might be nice to be close with her.

DREW. I guess that's true.

DAVIS. And Chelsea! She's probably going to need a lot of help with the baby soon, so the more people around, the better.

DREW. I can do that... Plus we have to make sure she knows what to name them.

DAVIS. ...What is she supposed to name them?

DREW. Tyler didn't tell you?

DAVIS. No...

    (**DREW** *smiles smugly.*)

Don't.

DREW. Okay.

    (*He sits for a moment.*)

...And can I hang out with you sometimes?

DAVIS. ...Sure.

DREW. I mean... I figured if Tyler liked you and he liked me then...we have to have something in common, right?

DAVIS. Yeah, for sure.

DREW. Okay good.

    (He smiles.)

We're gonna be really good gay dads.

DAVIS. What?

DREW. Godfathers!! I meant godfathers...

    (Awkward.)

I'm gonna go see if they're outside.

DAVIS. Please do.

    *(**DREW** walks to the door and opens it. Before leaving, he turns.)*

DREW. Tyson or Tyla. You can tell her.

    (He exits.)

    *(**DAVIS** sits alone on the couch for a minute. He begins to stand up, then sees Addy lying on the couch. He picks her up...then hugs her close to his chest. He takes a few deep breaths, then shrinks to the floor in tears, clutching the doll more desperately. **TYLER** enters and watches him from upstage left.)*

Scene Five

> (**SHANA** *enters from the outside door on stage right.*)

SHANA. Davis? We're outside and ready to –

> (*She stops and sees the doll in his hand.*)

...Are you okay?

> (**DAVIS**' *crying continues. She approaches him closer.*)

(*Gently.*) ...Davis, it's time to go.

DAVIS. I don't want to.

SHANA. You said you would, remember? We're all going to stand for your friend together.

DAVIS. I don't want to go anymore.

SHANA. You have to get up now, okay? ...Davis, I need you to get up now.

> (*He doesn't.*)

Ms. Evans is behind me and she's going to be upset if she finds you like this.

DAVIS. I don't care.

> (**FANNIE** *enters.*)

SHANA. Davis –

FANNIE. ...What's going on?

SHANA. He won't –

FANNIE. Davis, get up.

DAVIS. No.

FANNIE. Don't say no to me.

> (*She walks to the other side of him.*)

Do you hear me? I said get up.

DAVIS. I won't.

FANNIE. Little boy, stop crying, and stand up.

SHANA. You have to stop crying.

DAVIS. He's dead.

FANNIE. I know he's dead. You know why he's dead. So you don't get to stay home and cry. You stand up for him, do you understand? Stand up for us. Stop crying.

(**TYLER** *begins approaching* **DAVIS** *slowly.*)

SHANA. Get up.

FANNIE. Before I give you somethin' to cry about. Right now.

SHANA. You have to get up.

FANNIE. Stop crying. Stand up.

SHANA. It's time to get up.

TYLER. Davis, get up.

(*Crouching down to him.*)

You have to stop crying.

DAVIS. ...But –

TYLER. I'm not asking. Do it now.

DAVIS. I don't think I –

TYLER. Yes you can. Right now, Davis.

(**DAVIS** *looks up at* **TYLER** *towering over him.* **TYLER** *nods to him.* **DAVIS** *puts Addy down, wipes his face, and stands up.*)

SHANA. (*Puts her hand out to him.*) ...Okay, let's go outside and –

FANNIE. Uh-uh. He knows how to walk.

(*She heads toward the door.*)

We'll be waiting for you outside.

(**SHANA** *and* **FANNIE** *exit.* **TYLER** *closes the door behind them while* **DAVIS** *swallows hard and puts on a brave face.*)

DAVIS. ...I'm ready. I'm listening.

TYLER. You have to go with them.

DAVIS. I know.

TYLER. You owe me.

DAVIS. I know.

TYLER. *(Teasing.)* I swear, I let go of the protest thing, but I'll be damned if you don't go to my vigil.

DAVIS. I'm going...

   (Beat.)

...And then you'll go to sleep, right?

   (The smile fades from **TYLER***'s face quickly.)*

TYLER. ...What does that mean?

DAVIS. When you came back the night you died you told me there were things you wanted me to do before you ran out of time. You want me to go to your memorial. I'm going. Is there anything else you want me to do?

TYLER. ...I'm not going to sleep.

DAVIS. You have to go to sleep.

TYLER. No I don't.

DAVIS. Tyler –

TYLER. I don't know what you're trying to do, but you're not getting rid of me that easy. We'll just...we'll figure out a way to make it work. You can invite Chelsea to live with us, and help her raise my baby. And it'll be like I'm raising the baby too because I'll be there. And it'll be like we're living the happily ever after you've always wanted. Like raising a family together! It'll be just like I'm –

DAVIS. Like what? Like you're what, Tyler? Like you're alive?

   (Beat.)

Sure...it'll be "like" that. It will be "like" we're raising a family together. It will be "like" you're still here. It will be "like" you didn't come home one night to tell me someone killed you.

TYLER. It'll be whatever I want! I spent too much time listening to you and everyone else tell me what it can't be. Well I'm saying it can!

DAVIS. That doesn't matter anymore.

TYLER. ...Yes it does.

DAVIS. That's what you're afraid of, right? That people won't know about any of that? Well you're right. They'll know your face and your name and what happened to you, but they won't actually remember you. They won't remember anything about your life that mattered to you. Only what happened.

TYLER. Stop it!

DAVIS. No matter how many vigils, how many pictures of you with birthday cake, or little ceremonies thrown together by college students, people aren't going to see what you want them to see, and I can't stop it.

TYLER. Shut up! Shut up, Davis!!

DAVIS. No. You are dead! You were kill– you were murdered. And no matter how long you spend "haunting the shit out of me," I can't make people remember anything more than that, even though, that is the ONE thing about you that I am trying to forget. And that's hell, Tyler, because the only thing, the ONLY thing worse than losing you, is having to look at you and know that you're not really here.

　　　(Beat.)

You're not here.

　　　(TYLER *looks hurt. Almost betrayed.)*

TYLER. …I am too here.

DAVIS. *(Swallow. Brave face.)* Is there anything else I can do for you, Tyler.

TYLER. *(Desperate.)* I'm still here, just as much as I was ever. And I deserve it. I have a right to stay as long as I want!

DAVIS. You can't. What else can I do for you.

TYLER. *(Grappling.)* I'M NOT DONE YET! I made people smile. I did more every day than half the people alive will do in their entire lives! I have so much more to do a-a-and now you're telling me I have to go because some idiot thought I shouldn't be here anymore?

DAVIS. Yes. Now WHAT would you like me to do?

(**TYLER** *is looking at* **DAVIS** *in disbelief. He's pleading, but* **DAVIS** *doesn't budge...* **TYLER** *slowly sinks down to the couch, defeated.*)

TYLER. ...You can't forget.

DAVIS. I know.

TYLER. I know everyone is going to start...but you of all people, you're not allowed to.

DAVIS. I won't.

TYLER. And you have to like...remind people. Okay?

DAVIS. I will.

TYLER. Good.

(*He sits and breathes deeply.*)

...I'm not tired.

(*Beat.*)

...I want to sleep but I'm not tired.

DAVIS. ...Give me a minute.

(*He walks to the other side of the room and grabs one of the records from the box. He places the record on the record player.* **FANNIE** *enters quietly and calmly from stage left and sits in a chair up on stage left of Tyler's couch. The same jazz song begins to play as* **FANNIE** *hums along.**)

(**TYLER** *sits back on the couch.*)

TYLER. Davis?

DAVIS. Yeah?

TYLER. I'm sorry for waking you up that night. I know how crabby you get when you don't get consecutive hours... but I didn't want your last memory of us to be fighting. You're not mad at me are you?

DAVIS. Not even a little bit.

TYLER. Good...

> *(He drifts off a little bit.)*

> **(CHELSEA** *and* **DREW** *enter from stage left.* **CHELSEA** *is carrying a pillow. She gently lifts* **TYLER**'s *head and places the pillow under it.* **DREW** *unties and removes* **TYLER**'s *shoes for him, and the two of them settle him in a laying position.)*

Oh, and Davis?

DAVIS. Yeah buddy?

TYLER. ...Promise me you won't actually marry a man named Brogen. I didn't want to say anything before, but –

DAVIS. *(Rolling his eyes, bitter but loving.)* It sounds kind of douchey. I know. I won't.

> **(CHELSEA** *and* **DREW** *sit upstage left.)*

TYLER. Okay good.

> *(He drifts off a little bit more.)*

> **(SHANA** *enters stage right, carrying Tyler's hoodie. She covers his upper body with it as a blanket, then stands upstage right.)*

Hey Davis?

DAVIS. Tyler.

TYLER. *(Becoming more overcome with sleepiness.)* I know... it's just... I just wanted to say. Even though the ending really sucked, and to be honest, I was hoping to go out saving a puppy from...

> *(Yawn.)*

A burning building or something like that... I think maybe...

DAVIS. What is it?

TYLER. ...This is a really good song. It was kind of worth it, right? Yeah. Yeah I don't regret it... I don't regret any of it.

DAVIS. *(Hands Addy to* TYLER.*)* Me neither.

TYLER. *(Snuggling with Addy and his hoodie, finally feeling "cozy.")* I loved it. I loved all of it.

> *(Another yawn.)*

Okay, I'm gonna let you go to sleep now

> *(He turns over and wraps himself in the blanket.)*

Goodnight, Davis.

> *(The music fades away as* FANNIE *continues to hum. Lights slowly go down on* SHANA, *then* DREW *and* CHELSEA, *then, finally, down on* FANNIE *[her hum continues].)*

DAVIS. ...Goodnight, Tyler.

> *(Lights go down on* DAVIS *as he exits. Lights are last to go down on* TYLER, *leaving him to finally get a good night's sleep.)*

End of Play